true love

ALSO BY SARAH GERARD

FICTION
Binary Star

NONFICTION
Sunshine State

true love

A NOVEL

SARAH GERARD

HARPER

An Imprint of HarperCollins*Publishers*

TRUE LOVE. Copyright © 2020 by Sarah Gerard. All rights reserved. Printed in the United States of America. No part of this book may be used or reproduced in any manner whatsoever without written permission except in the case of brief quotations embodied in critical articles and reviews. For information, address HarperCollins Publishers, 195 Broadway, New York, NY 10007.

HarperCollins books may be purchased for educational, business, or sales promotional use. For information, please email the Special Markets Department at SPsales@harper collins.com.

FIRST EDITION

Designed by Elina Cohen

Library of Congress Cataloging-in-Publication Data has been applied for.

ISBN 978-0-06-293743-8

20 21 22 23 24 LSC 10 9 8 7 6 5 4 3 2 1

FOR PATTY COTTRELL

true love

My mother reached out to me again this morning, trying to reconcile. Odessa asks me what I would say to her if I could say anything. "I guess I would thank her for teaching me to be so kind," I say. I put her on speakerphone and hold my camera up to my crotch. I send Brian a picture with my underwear pulled to the side. My bedroom looms in the background.

It's been three years since I've spoken with my mother, since she said to me: "Why don't you cut yourself, take some pills, starve yourself, drop out of school, and suck some dick, Nina?" I had just told her I was considering not returning to college. I was two months out of rehab, talking to her on my bicycle en route to my second job as a line cook at the Pizza Shack. I told her never to contact me again.

You're my only child. You know I love you, she said in her email. *You've learned so much about yourself since then. You've had a difficult recovery.* She said we could resolve our differences on my terms. She offered to come back to St. Petersburg.

"Have you responded?" says Odessa.

"No."

"Are you going to?"

I touch myself and send Brian a picture of the gloss on my fingertips. "I don't know why she would come here if she knows I'm leaving in a month," I say. I place my fingers in my mouth.

"How would she know that?"

"She talks to my dad."

I imagine Brian wheeling over to the senior editor in his chair. Having to cross his legs.

He texts me. **You're killing me.**

"Hang on," I say to Odessa.

You should touch yourself, I type.

"What are you waiting for her to say to you?" she says. "Isn't this what you wanted?"

I'm at work, says Brian.

So go to the bathroom.

"Yeah," I say, "I just don't think she's sincere."

Odessa has known her since we were five. I expect her to agree with me. She's quiet. A picture of Brian's dick appears on my phone. It's thick and curved, with trimmed hair, dark and tight against his groin. He snapped the photo in the mirror of an employee bathroom. It's lit from above.

Are you making yourself cum? I say.

You should help me, he says.

"Hang on, Odessa," I say. "Seth is texting me."

"No worries."

Brian and I make plans for him to pick me up at eight. This gives me a few hours to file my article with him about the ongoing effects of the Deepwater Horizon oil spill. If I have time after that, I'll read *Numina* submissions and wash my pussy.

"Let me call you later," I say to Odessa. "He just asked me to help him with something."

"Okay." She hangs up.

BRIAN ARRIVES AT eleven. I meet him down the street and climb into his black Jetta. He offers no explanation for how late he is, but carries on a side conversation as he drives, holding his phone down by his left thigh. We pass Seth's apartment, where a gauzy white bedsheet hangs in the window, illuminated by the light over his worktable. I imagine him smoking weed, listening to Kurt Vile, painting color studies in his sketchbook. He texted me just as Brian arrived and invited me over. I was disappointed by his tenderness, his willingness to have me in his space. It makes me look like a bad person.

We park down the street from the beach and walk hand in hand down the brick road, past craftsman houses cloaked in darkness. We cross the last road to the Gulf of Mexico and are met with the sulfurous stench of red tide. We look out at the water, but it's too dark to see the fish kills lying along the shore. Brian turns toward me and lifts my shirt to find the small of my back. My body lights up. I realize I've stopped breathing and inhale, coughing at the smell. He pulls me over to a dune, and I kneel to take him in my mouth.

IT'S PAST MIDNIGHT when he drops me off at Seth's apartment. The light above the worktable is off, but the light beside his chaise is on, which means he's reading. I take the alley down the side of his building, past the group home for teenage mothers, so I can enter from the back to give him the idea that I've walked to his house from my own.

I cross the crushed-shell parking lot and climb a set of sun-bleached wooden stairs. I knock on his kitchen window. The warm light from his bedroom spills down the hall when he opens the door. He moves to let me in. "Odessa said you told her you were helping me with something," he says.

"I didn't want to talk on the phone anymore and I didn't want to hurt her feelings," I say.

"What were you doing?"

"Finishing an article."

He closes the door behind me and gestures toward his room. "I walked by your apartment and didn't see a light on."

"I might have been in the bath."

He's covered the rugs with plastic tarps. A vertical canvas, recently primed, leans against the wall atop a waist-high bookshelf of tattered monographs. He's pulled out two by Richard Diebenkorn and Gerhard Richter and laid them open on the worktable. Several color-field paintings lean together against another shelf of paperbacks.

I sit on the chaise longue. "What were you doing so late at the gallery?" I say. As the artist-in-residence at Black Box, Seth is paid for nine hours of work there every week, but as it happens, he ends up working almost forty. Last week, I went with him to the home of the gallery's owner. Their conversation centered on small-town gossip, gallery business, and light flirtation of the kind gay men employ with straight men. Seth reciprocated and deflected, ever aware that his reputation, his future, and his self-image were in Theo's hands. My mind was two mirrors facing each other. I pretended to be absorbed by Theo's collection of African diaspora art. I wasn't actually engaged until Theo asked me about my progress on the inaugural issue of *Numina*, the gallery's flagship publication, which Seth volunteered me to edit. "People are submitting," I told Theo. "I'd be happy to go over it with you this week." It's clear he continues to hope that I'm temporary, two years after meeting me. He refers to me sarcastically as Dorothy Parker. "That would be fine," he said.

Seth closes the monographs. "Theo entrusted me with the de-installation of the emerging artist show," he says. "Taking down a show involves removing artwork from the walls, wrapping it properly for shipping, patching the walls, repainting them, mopping the floors. It's not glamorous, but it affords me time for contemplation."

"What were you contemplating?"

"The situation I find myself in."

He swirls a paintbrush in a yogurt container filled with water. He taps it gently on the brim and lays it on a paper towel.

"A studio practice utilizes various discoveries," he says. "My recent discovery is that direct confrontation leads to a personal clarification of environmental relations. The most urgent themes in art break down barriers between people. Yet a studio is a place of isolation. A contradiction. And in the present period, my studio practice is not solitary."

"Are you saying you want me to leave?"

"I don't believe that's what I said."

"I'm not sure what you're saying."

"The polemic push of the organism against the uncontrolled dynamics of his environment can be very generative."

I look at him.

"What were you doing tonight, Nina?" he says.

"Writing in the bathtub," I say.

"I knocked and you didn't answer."

"Sorry about that. I was wearing headphones. Would you like to hear what I was writing?"

"Sure."

I take my phone from my purse. In my email, I find the latest finished story in the Ira Cycle, my new series of thinly veiled meditations on my relationship with Seth, which I began after abandoning my novel. This story is called "An Opening." In it, Ira has invited Liz to an opening at the art gallery where he works, and has hung a solo show of his paintings. A nice-sized gathering has convened on the space, among them his high school art teacher and the gallery's owner. He's introducing Liz to a small group of people, but is describing her as a friend and new collaborator rather than his girlfriend, though they have been dating for almost two years and have never collaborated on a project. Liz is playing along. She doesn't want to contradict and embarrass him, or humiliate herself, and though she wants to be known as his girlfriend, it is also validating to be described as an artist.

Afterward, Liz stays at Ira's apartment. They spoon on a chaise longue, which functions as his bed, in his bedroom, which is also his studio. Ira acquired the chaise longue for twenty dollars at a yard sale. The original fabric is worn through, so he's tucked layers of blankets around it rather than repair it. When they share it, Liz is trapped against the wall, so she can't turn or stretch or adjust her position. She is never comfortable, and always wakes in pain, but she would rather be in pain than sleep alone. Ira never stays at her apartment. He can't paint there.

She disappears in the morning before he wakes. She knows he would be annoyed to find her there. He would solemnly make her toast, as if it's his duty. *Ira's bedroom window faces east*, she writes in her journal. *The sun shines on him every morning when I leave him.*

"Is that a threat?" he says when I finish.

"What do you mean?"

He snickers. I light the roach in his ashtray. Outside, headlights streak past on the freeway on-ramp. Gulls take flight from the guardrail. Four Post-its taped to the window correspond to miniature empty canvases beneath them: *EPIC VOID, PREGNANT SPACE, EMPTY HOLE, HOLLOW LOT.*

"I passed a mother and two young children this morning on Ninth Avenue petting a dead squirrel," I say.

"How maudlin."

"Isn't she worried about disease?"

"Some people aren't." He smiles at me, then pulls his shirt over his head and drops it on the tarp at his feet, where he also deposits his underwear. He disappears into the bathroom and takes a long shower while I wait. When he emerges, he smells like tea tree and Fast Orange. His long hair drips down his back. "You can stay here, but I can't guarantee you'll enjoy it," he says.

"Why not?"

"Because I'm not going to sleep with you."

"You think that's why I'm here?"

"I think physical intimacy is more important to you than it is to me."

He sits beside me. I undress and press myself against the wall, and he lies down in front. I wrap my arm around him and lower my face into his hair.

"I know you love me," he says.

two

I began cutting myself and sneaking pills in middle school, resentful, bored, and unsupervised. I suspected my feelings were more intense than other people's. My parents were preoccupied with their mutual hatred of each other, inspired by the acrimonious divorce and my mother's new residence in a trailer park in Lutz. She has since moved to a nudist colony in Kissimmee to live with her polycule.

I moved to New York for college. I stole Adderall from my suitemate. I fucked her boyfriend on a weekly basis. I fucked people without condoms. I especially liked men who already had girlfriends. The hope was always that they'd leave their girlfriends for me; for them to leave their girlfriends would have been the ultimate victory, proof of my irresistibility, but they never did.

I believe it was my suitemate who called my father upon the advice of other students whose identities remain a mystery to me. I lived for eight weeks in a Tampa facility named after one of the twelve steps. My official diagnosis was drug addiction, but I was never picky, and any numbing or mood-altering agent would do. Weed, wine, sex, starvation. I signed up for trauma counseling because I felt something had happened to me, although I was unable to articulate a single event. Others in the group shared stories of incest, combat, rape, dead children.

I became infatuated with a Kevin Spacey look-alike in facility-wide group therapy. He sat across from me and never looked at me, but I felt we had a connection that ran deeper than flirting. We were warned not to start a new relationship until after a year of sobriety. I never said more than two words to him, but I continued masturbating to his memory until he called me one morning, a month after I'd left. I'd never given him my number. Hearing his voice, I remembered that he had a family. He had stolen his daughter's Girl Scout money for meth. He'd hired prostitutes on business trips to Thailand.

IT'S SWARMING SEASON, and my building is infested with termites. I awake to their wings beating against my cheekbones. I gather some into a plastic lunch bag to bring to my landlord, who has insisted she needs to see a "living sample." My duplex neighbor composts in a plastic trash can five feet from my back door. I drag the can in front of their sunporch screen and ride my bicycle to the hypnotist's office.

"My mother disappeared and my father was always working," I tell her. I've been seeing the hypnotist on a sliding scale for the last month because I have a deep intuition that something is wrong with me, somehow related to my unnameable trauma, and hypnosis seems compatible with my daily wake-and-bake habit. She is white, in her late forties, with dreadlocks and carved wooden gauges weighing down her ears. The henna on her hands looks like Spanish moss, and her office is plush with amber lighting, palo santo, and embroidered pillows. She told me in our first session that after ten years of working with children in foster care, and five years in disaster relief, this is the field where she feels she can make the most difference. "I wish I could offer it for free," she said.

"I'd have a babysitter three or four nights a week, and it was always some teenager who would invite her boyfriend over," I say. "I'd call boys in my class who didn't want to talk to me, who would answer the phone and hear my voice and hang up. Sometimes there were friends, but everyone eventually leaves me. When I moved back to Florida, none of my college friends even called me."

AFTER REHAB, I attended NA for two weeks, then hooked up with a crust punk I met smoking outside after a meeting one night. The topic had been loneliness. I was gazing at a light fixture where moth after moth incinerated itself. "I'm an only child, too," he said to me, bumming a cigarette. Though drawing him closer into my emotional sphere seemed risky at that critical stage in my sobriety, I couldn't bring myself to prefer being alone after that. I couldn't find it in me to reject him when he'd shown me such kindness as to ask me for a lighter.

I moved him in with me. He began smoking crack again, but I couldn't kick him out because then he'd be homeless. This went on for weeks, until I met Seth riding my bicycle home from the Pizza Shack. He was two blocks from my apartment, unloading bags from the back of the gallery's pickup. I recognized him as a moody artist from my high school. He invited me upstairs to drink tea, and a week later, we fucked on his mite-crawling rag rugs. I continued fucking him for another month until I worked up the nerve to dump Mission. Mission skipped town to go train-hopping again. Seth has never let me forget this series of events, even two years later. Whenever he can, he subtly alludes to "the way I live my life."

"SETH DOESN'T TRUST me," I tell the hypnotist. "It's his Lutheran upbringing and his parents' divorce, and then, of course, his dad died. Hit by a Mack truck. I think he blames his mother on some level and, by extension, all women. I don't know how to leave him, or if I should, or how I even could, or how I can fix things between us. He's moving to New York with me, which seems to suggest he loves me."

"You love him," she says.

"Yes."

"Love is a trance."

"Is that a song?"

"A trance is an 'inwardly directed, selectively focused attention.' It's a story in which you become so absorbed you can't see anything else." She opens a drawer to her left and removes a smudge stick. She lights it and waves it back and forth until the smell of sage fills the room.

"Pretend you're alone," she says.

She's obscured behind a curtain of smoke.

"THEY'RE ORCHIDS," SETH told me that first day upstairs. He was reading my mind, brewing tea in a thick jar. He set a timer on the kitchen counter in a beam of late afternoon light. The room was dense with tendrils of hanging flowers, which I'd been admiring. "They're not always the most beautiful, but they have bilateral symmetry, so when they bloom, they look like human faces. They watch you."

He kept his eyes downcast, then looked directly into mine. He was taller than me by almost a foot, so I tilted my chin up to him. His cotton shirt was worn through, nearly transparent. "Do you smoke weed?" he said, inviting me to sit on the rug while he sketched. He passed the joint down to me. Chrysanthemums bloomed in the golden water of my jar. The sound of him enchanted me; his confidence convinced me he was wise. "What is art, Nina?" he asked me. "I still am not sure. What faculties does it command? Which aspects of our humanity, of ourselves? It may be easy to talk about, but it's hard to accept. What do I want out of it? Where do I want to go with it?"

He turned on a lecture by Alan Watts, and talked alongside or over it for my benefit, filling in the details for my full understanding. The topic, coincidentally, was how to attract your soul mate. "On the deepest level, a person on the whole can get in the way of his own existence," Watts said.

I found myself telling him about the novel I was writing. I asked him if he would read it and give me feedback. I'd begun drafting it in my notebook when I'd moved back to Florida, disconnected from the internet and unsure of what else to do with my sobriety. The story followed a college student who'd been forced to go to rehab. I brought him a copy the next day in an orange envelope. I'd written the title on the front and signed my name underneath.

"I'd like you to model nude for me sometime," he said, taking the envelope. He held me with his gaze. "If you would be comfortable with that."

"A TRANCE SHAPES what we see and how we respond," says the hypnotist. She hands me a tiny bottle of water and a tissue. I've drooled on myself. "We're highly receptive, much like when we're in love. It's debatable whether we even have full use of our judgment or our faculties."

She tells me I need to work on my self-esteem; then she leads me through an intervention that involves tapping various parts of my body, repeating a mantra. I leave with a recording of our session that she's burned onto a CD, which I have no way of playing. I notice

I've been in her office for two hours. "Please don't apologize," she says. "I enjoy it as much as you do."

On the way home, I bike past Seth's apartment. His window is open. He doesn't answer the door, which doesn't mean he isn't home. He could be in there choosing isolation. I sit and wait for him.

WHEN I RETURNED to model for Seth in the nude, I was surprised to find that our high school art teacher was there in his studio, drinking wine. The Stone Roses were playing in the room's half darkness. I sat next to Mr. Kruck, a clean, gentle gay man. We were silent, as if bewitched by the presence of Seth, a sort of modern oracle. "I hear you're a novelist now," Mr. Kruck whispered. I couldn't tell if he was amused. His eyes were fixed on the development of Seth's abstract masterpiece.

"That's my book," I said, gesturing to the orange envelope, unopened on the floor near a stack of *Artforum*.

"Extraordinary. Seth, what can you tell me about this future bestseller?" he said.

"Nothing," said Seth. "I haven't read it."

"You'll have to fill him in once you do," I said. He looked at me, then turned back around and continued painting.

"I'm not sure I can give you a proper critique, Nina," he said. "I would like your permission to pass it on to my friend Jared. He's a student of literature."

"Yes, a wonderful idea," said Mr. Kruck.

"You know him?" I said.

"Oh, yes. He was your classmate."

Seth washed his paintbrush and laid it on a towel. He selected a pencil from a box of drawing supplies and scribbled on the back of a receipt. "This will depend on his other commitments," he said. "But here's his number. I'll tell you when to text him, if he agrees. He prefers to text."

When Mr. Kruck left, Seth resumed explicating his work in progress. "I feel that negative space and form play important recent roles. I transmute proportions of negative space onto dissimilar arbitrary portions of canvas. Thereby I explore space in painting, in particular the oppositional forces caught in the openness of absence."

I lingered. He disappeared into the bathroom adjacent to his bedroom, and I heard him brushing his teeth. He emerged in his boxers, wearing glasses, as if ready for bed.

"So, when do you want to start?" I said.

He squinted.

"The modeling."

"Oh. I'm sorry, I don't have time tonight."

"I see."

"The demands on my time are immense. The real world steals my sanity. Here I am, constantly surveilled and manipulated by technology, reality and advertising alike pissing in my face. You understand."

I, too, often felt attacked, put upon, pushed around. I couldn't help but feel as if only I could love Seth enough for him to be fully open, and that only he could lend me the recognition I so needed. Falling in love with Seth was a way of falling in love with myself.

I WAIT FOR an hour for him to return or emerge; then I leave, wondering if he's watching me through the window. I once waited four hours at a bar where he'd told me to meet him before deciding he'd stood me up. He'd forgotten. Agreements mean nothing to him. If he actually moves to New York with me, I'm convinced it will be an accident. He doesn't answer his phone if he's "working." He won't respond to texts. Days will go by and I will hear nothing from him. "I'm not married to my call log," he tells me. I feel like an animal. Begging.

I'm a block from my duplex when a cat darts from beneath a car and runs in front of my tire. I swerve to avoid hitting it and fly over the handlebars, landing on my shoulder. I skid several feet on my face and lie on my stomach, scanning for injuries. I watch the cat watching me bleed. A silver-dollar-sized abrasion turns red on my elbow. I roll to my side and gather my bike. I limp to the grass.

I sit, assessing the damage. The dry grass is like tiny blades cutting into my thighs. The front tire is out of true. I wonder vaguely whether I have a concussion, but seem unable to fully form the question. I sit for a long time and consider napping, just for a minute. The block is family houses. Someone will see me if I die.

The cat approaches and rubs against me. I push it away. It rubs me again and catches my bleeding arm with its tail. The pain starts me awake, and I push the cat, harder, then look at it, suddenly sorry. It's skinny, flea-infested, its paws matted with tar. A Creamsicle tabby. It looks like my childhood cat Skittles. Skittles died tragically of renal failure when I was fifteen. I have always blamed myself for failing to notice sooner that she was sick.

I swear under my breath and decide I'm not going to cry. I resent Seth for failing to be here to help me. I peel myself from the ground and lean against the bike. The cat follows me for a block and then walks in front of my foot. I stop to avoid kicking her. I squat and look at her more closely. Her eyes are clear blue. I pick her up and carry her against my chest.

three

Soon after the aborted drawing session, Jared invited me to his home. I arrived in the early evening, chained my bike to his fence on the brick street, and proceeded up the paving stone walkway through a sandy garden of wilting bromeliads. The house was Spanish-style, eggshell-colored, with a screened-in side porch. An old bathtub filled with potting soil housed weeds. Jared answered the door shirtless. He wore a knee-length floral skirt. His hair was pulled into a bun, and a tattoo of Hokusai's *The Great Wave off Kanagawa* covered his left shoulder. "Welcome, Nina," he said. "Come in."

The entrance was partially lit by an antique floor lamp draped in red silk. I eyed the bookshelf and recognized many of the authors I'd read in my undergraduate gender studies and African American literature seminars. Through an open bedroom door, I could see a man with a Jew 'fro sleeping beside a skinny white woman covered in stick-and-poke tattoos.

"So, you're a writer?" I said to Jared.

"I'm an artist. One of my media is text."

"What are your other mediums?"

"Media. Carpentry. You may have seen some of my work at Black Box."

"Did you have a show?"

"I made the benches."

We proceeded past the open bedroom and onto the porch, where an old corduroy sofa shared space with a particleboard coffee table, a grill, a dusty workbench, and several unopened cardboard boxes sagging under stale rainwater. It was carpeted pool table green.

"Tell me about your writing," Jared said. He opened a cigar box on the coffee table. It held four Swisher Sweets, a sandwich bag of dry shake, an X-Acto knife, and a lighter. I sat on the couch.

"What do you want to know?"

"Whatever you see fit to tell me."

"Well, the book is loosely based on my life."

"I had wondered."

"But I mean, it's fiction."

"What's true and what's not?"

"None of it is technically true."

He rolled the blunt silently as I watched. He licked it, dragged his thumb lengthwise down the paper, spun it, then stuck the whole of it in his mouth and pulled it out again.

"I look forward to talking with you about your novel," he said. "First, I need to pass some items along to a friend who has just arrived."

A black Beetle pulled into the driveway. A petite Latina climbed out of it. She wore pinup shoes, black-and-white polka-dotted shorts, and a lime halter top. She teetered up the walkway and across the yard.

"Hang on, Claudette, let me get them," said Jared. "Excuse me for a moment," he said to me.

"No problem."

The woman opened the screen door and held her hand out for me to shake it. There was something hostile in the gesture. "How do you know Jared?" she said.

"Seth introduced us."

"Why?"

"I'm a writer," I said for the first time. "Jared is reading my novel."

She looked at Jared. He was just returning with a shopping bag of women's lingerie, which he handed to her.

"No, Claudette," he told her, reading her face. "She's sleeping with Seth."

"We should hang out sometime." She smiled. She seemed to be saying this for Jared more than me. I listened as she segued into a story about a love triangle at the coffee shop where, I gathered, she and Jared both worked. The full version involved a lot of characters, some of whom were as yet unidentified. Jared sensed that I was waiting and lit the blunt. He passed it to me on the couch. I passed it back to him. With the blunt, we were passing back and forth the understanding that Claudette was intruding on a conversation that was only just beginning.

He took out his phone and nodded to show her that he was listening. He began to move his thumbs across the screen. Claudette continued. She was speculating about the possibility of the coffee shop's management disapproving of staff affairs. Whether it was possible the owner would fire someone. She didn't seem to care that Jared was openly talking to someone else while she was talking to him. I took my phone out of my purse and texted Seth a heart emoji. I kept my hand on top of the phone afterward in case he responded. It vibrated.

Nina, your ideas are good but you let them stew too much upstairs without getting out and getting examined. Many of your sentences are long and awkward. Your metaphors are frequently mixed, and lose potency as a result. Your voice is good, but gets muddled and lost when you reach for big ideas. You rely too much on staid literary mechanisms that no longer have currency. You have a tendency to tell instead of showing. Unresolved plot holes and inconsistencies riddle the story line, though you do some skilled foreshadowing. The story attempts to be at once gritty realism and patent romanticism, but ends up being effectively neither, while its overblown descriptions of good and evil give it a moralizing tone. This story feels raw, like it hasn't gone through a drafting process yet. You seem not to be able to see the forest for the trees, and there are some lovely trees, but they just don't make a forest. You obviously have a good grasp of language, but you need to work on some of the basic nuts and bolts of storytelling before attempting to build anything as grand as you're doing, otherwise its structural integrity cannot hold up even a well-wrought facade. Things you can work on include: making your world logically consistent; making sure all things, actions, places, and names have both context and causation; getting rid of unnecessary verbiage, especially words whose duty is being done by other words; working to eliminate clichés and overused literary mechanisms; and using the right word instead of several close approximations all lumped together.

I closed my phone and returned it to my purse. I stared at the arm of the sofa while Claudette finished her story. It took her ten or fifteen minutes. I sank into my body. I felt at once far away and painfully present. I considered the attractiveness of vanishing. I would leave Jared's porch, walk to the water, and continue walking until I was submerged.

Claudette reminded Jared about dinner at her mother's house tomorrow. "I love you," she said.

"You, too, kid," he said.

They kissed.

"Bye, Nina," she said, as if we were friends.

He watched her drive away, but remained looking out at the darkening street after her car had turned the corner, as if deep in thought. "Sorry about that," he said.

"That's okay."

"Did you have any questions for me?"

"Not really."

He seemed offended. "I've read your novel. I am the only one who's read it aside from you. There's nothing you want to know?"

"You've given me a lot to think about."

"I see." He lit the blunt, which was now a wet roach. He burned his fingers and reached inside the wooden box for a clip. He held the metal end of it and passed it to me.

"I guess I have one question," I said. "What do you write?"

"Everything is writing," he said. "At the moment, I'm working on my Bumble profile."

I'M ONCE AGAIN stoned on Jared's porch. His roommate is out selling drugs to teenagers getting drunk at the Bends, Seth is at a Black Box show opening, and I have the night off. Over the two years since I met him, my friendship with Jared has become strategic. It normalizes me to Seth by giving Jared the opportunity to approve of me. It enables him to explain me to Seth at key moments. And it gives me someone other than Seth to cry to when Seth ghosts me. While maintaining that, due to seniority, his first loyalty is to Seth, Jared also validates my frustration when Seth says things like, "I hope you know that the time I give you is not time I already have."

Importantly, Jared encouraged me to finish my last twelve credits at the community college. "Don't do it because you're told to," he said. "Do it because journalism is dying." He proofread my applications to MFA programs. When I was accepted, he was instrumental in convincing Seth to move with me to New York.

I treat Jared as if he's someone I can confide in, though he isn't always; he's a gossip. But, as he says, "Trust is an action."

At the moment, Jared is mansplaining polyamory, and I am performing compassion through active listening.

"If Claudette is uncomfortable, then she and I need to talk about that," he says. "It does me no good if she talks to other people. I've been honest with her about my expectations and involvements with other women." He passes the blunt.

"My understanding is that this complicates her relationship with Sofia," I say.

"And of course I feel badly about that," he says.

"But this is how you're made."

"I am the way I am, and she chooses to be with me, knowing who I am."

Jared doesn't reveal his other paramours to one another unless they ask him using specific names, as in "Are you fucking Sofia?" This is necessary to preserve everyone's privacy. Otherwise, he has a difficult time forming connections with people, and forming connections is what he naturally does as a polyamorous person. *"Homo sapiens are not biologically inclined to monogamy,"* he says, citing the landmark pop science book *Sex at Dawn*. To restrict this part of himself is equivalent to torture. "I am capable of feeling deep love for more than one person at a time. Haven't you ever wanted to be with someone who wasn't your partner?"

I wouldn't admit this to him. I also wonder if he isn't sending a coded message—if he wasn't watching me with Brian on the beach a few weeks ago. We're only, at this moment, two blocks from the location where he came on my face in the dunes. My neutral expression asserts that it wasn't me he saw, just in case it was.

"This is a touchy subject for me," I say, "because of my mom."

"Right, the unicorn."

"Please don't say that."

"Have you met any of her partners?"

"No."

"What's your relationship like with her?"

SINCE LEAVING FOR college, I've only seen my mother a handful of times. This occasion stands as an exemplar: I was home for Thanksgiving and asked if I could come to Lutz, an hour from my dad's. I didn't want to drive all the way out there, but I knew I'd have to if I wanted to see her. I was on my cell in my father's kitchen while he shouted at Bill Maher from the living room.

"I'm not asking for pity, but it really sucks to be me some days," she explained. "I don't have the time or energy to talk about it. It's just hard for me to host people. I don't have the space or the time to clean for you."

I apologized. She complained that her work schedule was punishing—my sense was that this was by design. She had been this way since leaving my father. As long as she worked upward of eighty hours a week, she never had to get close to people, and she would always have something or someone to gripe about.

"That's both-sides-ism, Bill!" my dad yelled.

"Hang on, Mom, let me step outside."

"Go far away so he doesn't yell at you," she said. This was supposed to be a joke about how my father was someone who yelled at me, except that he wasn't. If she made him my enemy, though, then she would have more of me, even from another city, even as she kept me at an uncloseable emotional distance.

"I don't want you to feel bad," I said, shutting the front door.

"It's just honestly really hard for me to have visitors or take time off work."

"It's easiest for me to come now because I'm in Florida."

"I can't commit to anything, Nina. I'm sorry."

HER TRAILER WAS in a park called Slash Pines. Mobile homes were near the street and RVs were in the back, near the swamp. My mother's home was somewhere in between. She'd left a key in a hanging planter on the porch, where she also kept her bicycle, a tiny refrigerator, and some dirty deck furniture. Inside was clean, the window air-conditioning unit turned down to sixty-nine, churning with two pine-tree-shaped car fresheners taped to the vent. The dust on her sewing machine suggested it wasn't used. Cases of liquor sat stacked against the refrigerator, her kitchen serving as extra storage for the bar where she worked. "I don't even drink," she'd told me, as if working in a bar was an ironic twist of fate that had befallen her—her, of all people.

I lay on her floral-print couch vaping and texting with my RA, Shower Dave. I only ever saw him leaving the men's communal bathroom wrapped in a towel. I hoped to sleep with him by the end of the semester. The competition was stiff among female residents on my floor. I sent him half a dozen thirst traps, and hours later, we had both cum repeatedly. By the time my mother came in, I couldn't pull out.

I try to maintain a healthy skepticism toward any organized system of thought, Dave was saying. We'd transitioned from sexting to falling in love. I'm glad I wasn't raised with a religion.

She was frowning, taking off her sneakers.

I'm the opposite, I said. I like being told what to do ;-)

"Who are you talking to?" she said, but proceeded into the tiny kitchen before I could answer. She left the lights off while she opened the cabinets.

"My roommate."

Let's test that theory, he said.

She extracted a jar of peanut butter and stood there, watching me as she ate it with a spoon.

My mom just got home, I said.

Is it crazy that I miss you?

Not crazy at all.

"How was work?" I said.

"Fine."

"What happened?"

"I'm not sure what you mean."

Send me a letter from Florida.

I will.

"What's up?" I said.

She threw out the plastic jar. It landed hollowly in the bottom of the trash can. She sat against the counter. "Nothing," she said.

"What's wrong?"

"Nothing, I just thought you wanted to see me."

SHE ASKED ME to leave by the middle of the next day.

"I just need this time alone before I work for twelve hours," she said, walking me to my father's car. "People take time off because they know I'll cover it and I won't complain," she said, hugging me. "Thanks for understanding."

"No worries, Mom. You should rest."

"I wish I could."

A MONTH LATER, she met the couple who would become her new family. They invited her to live with them in the nudist colony, and by Christmas, for the first time since flying me to college, she invited me down for winter break. I'm sure she did so knowing I wouldn't come.

"You know my mind works so quickly," she said, praising her new polycule's generosity, their openness, their radical acceptance. "I'm very blunt, I talk quickly, it's just how quickly my mind works, and I'm not a bullshitter. They're the only people I've ever met who can keep up with me."

I was happy for her.

When my father learned about her relationship, the first since they'd separated, he plunged into a depression that lasted for months. There were days of him not answering his phone. When he did, he was slow, as if drunk. "I know you don't like her," he told me. "I know that I left her. You know that I had to. But your mother is the only woman I've ever loved."

IT'S AFTER MIDNIGHT. Jared's head is in my lap on the porch, lit orange by a streetlight. A skink slips through a hole in the screen, then tries to find its way out again but can't, and slithers into shadow. The pulse of the darkness closes in, and I realize I've waited too long to walk home, that I will need to ask Jared to drive me. A mosquito lands on the back of my hand, and I watch it suck me, detached but fascinated. I kill it.

Jared's breathing has slowed, but he wakes with my movement, and I comb my fingers through his hair.

"I'm just curious," I say, as he opens his eyes. "What if you and I wanted to fuck?"

He considers it. He rubs his face with his palm. "I would talk to Seth about it," he says.

"I'm surprised."

"As you know, he's never been open to any kind of nonmonogamy, ethical or otherwise." He sits up. "It's his upbringing. He doesn't espouse Lutheranism, but he takes comfort in its traditions."

"It's frustrating."

"It's up to you whether or not you want to accommodate him. I've talked to Seth about polyamory. He does listen. He's just a very fearful person. Trauma has lasting effects."

"I'm aware."

"His parents divorced and his father died less than a year later."

"Is it always about that?"

"In some ways, that's when Seth stopped maturing."

four

When I don't respond to her email, my mother begins texting me.

Happy birthday, Nina! she says. I'm so proud of the strong, confident woman you've become. We're constantly changing and evolving. Cheers to many more years of growth and learning.

I'm sorry I haven't reached out. I know I've been distant for a long time and I feel like a terrible mother. I just went to the beach and remembered how we used to look for sand dollars together. You were always so good at finding them! Love you, dear daughter.

Remember that I love you, dear daughter! Don't ever forget that you are loved!

I hope you're having a wonderful day! I miss you!

MY MOTHER IS the only person who has ever hit me in the face. I was eight and we were walking back from the public pool. I had finally learned to swim. In the past, when my mother has guilted me about my life choices, she has found it useful to remind me that she "taught me how to swim," conveniently ignoring that it was mandatory for children to take swimming lessons in Florida public schools at the time.

It was summer and the sun was directly overhead. I had been taking swimming lessons at summer camp for three years already. But I wasn't a strong swimmer and I was happy, finally able to tread water for sixty seconds or more, excited that this new skill would be rewarded with ice cream. This was before Breyers became "frozen dairy dessert."

I was swinging my bathing suit in a circle, stupidly. It made a sound like *thwack!* when it hit her—I didn't know what had happened. Before I could apologize, she hauled off and decked me.

I fell on the sidewalk. I sat looking at how it sparkled. She told me that I would have to lie to my father about the black eye.

We never talked about it, and she never apologized or explained herself, and it never happened again, physically. Those who know her know that beneath her anger is tenderness, and beneath her tenderness is fury. She's the youngest of three children, with two older brothers. She had to learn at a young age how to defend herself. "She's the most difficult person in my life," my uncle Jude once told me.

IT'S THREE WEEKS before the move, and my father asks to see me. I bring Odessa as a buffer, and Odessa brings her twelve-year-old, Maxima. Max is genderqueer, but they haven't told their mother, and their mother still uses feminine pronouns—Odessa thinks nonbinaryism and transgenderism are trends, and says things like, "Is everyone gay now?" and, "I wouldn't know what to do down there." She tells Max, "What's mine is yours and what's yours is mine." I've tried to complexify and resist this idea in private with Max, but it's hard to explain to a middle schooler how they're their own person.

It's half an hour to the beach condo, where we hope my father will feed us. A storm is blowing in from the Gulf. It could wash the red tide out or spread it around; there's no predicting. They've identified the culprit as chemical runoff from agriculture and phosphorous mining. Greed selling us out in Tallahassee. It could take months to dissipate, and there's nothing they can do to speed it up. You can't Monistat the ocean.

We park beneath the stilted building and climb the stairs to the second floor, looking out over the churning, rust-colored water. Some diehards are out there in the shallows. Disgusting. My father answers in his work slacks with his shirt open and a bottle of cold-brew coffee in hand. Since recovering from my mother's midlife crisis, he's become a serial dieter, obsessed with wellness. "I'm no longer consuming free radicals," he told me on the phone last night. Apparently these are unpaired electrons that cause oxidative stress. Now he's on a low-carb, high-antioxidant diet, of mostly nuts and berries. He looks fragile and bewildered, like a bird. The room smells pleasantly rancid, and it turns out he's composting in a mini dumpster on the kitchen counter. I would say that my father needs to get laid, but he's learned to be too happy alone.

He sinks into his calfskin recliner. Everything in his house looks brand-new, like he just remodeled. There's something on his mind, I can tell by the way he adjusts his position, but instead of speaking it aloud, he changes the channel on the HDTV. Odessa and Max sit beside me on the Boca do Lobo sofa, and we all commence watching the last episode of the first half of the last season of *Mad Men*. My father likes *Mad Men* because he, too, used to be a drunk, over-the-hill ad exec watching the world leave him behind, and he remembers the sixties being an easier time for white men like him.

"Your mother called me," he says, looking at me.

"I don't want to see her."

"You don't have to."

"She's not moving back. It's a test to see if I'll stay here for her. She knows that I'm moving."

He smiles at the television. "I'm not arguing."

Odessa watches Max navigate to the page on their Instagram where they can see what their friends are liking.

"What?" they say to her.

"Why is Violet liking Jorden's posts?"

Violet is Max's girlfriend, but I've promised not to share this with Odessa. She thinks they're best friends. "Consider that your mother may be a closet lesbian," I told Max. "Maybe it would be good for her to see you living authentically."

"Didn't Jorden call you a retard?" Odessa says.

"In fifth grade."

"That was only two years ago."

Odessa was thirteen when she had Maxima. For the first ten years of Max's life, Odessa was still a child. They lived with her mother, an ultraconservative cunt rag. It's only recently that Odessa has been able to afford an apartment where they can live alone. They still share a bed, so when guys sleep over, Max moves to the sofa.

I barely talked to Odessa while I was in New York. It's only since moving back to Florida that she and I have grown close again. My hypnotist has asked me why I continue to feel that I can extend myself to her, if I feel I'm in any way able to help her, or if there's another reason why I let her in close to me. Does it mean that I'm compassionate? Do I have poor boundaries? Am I codependent? Am I infantilizing her? Am I in love with her?

"Do you want me to talk to Violet?" she says. "I won't say anything about you. I'll just be like, 'How do you know Jorden?'"

"I would rather you didn't."

"I adopted a cat from the street," I say.

"How sweet," says my dad.

"Do you want to see a picture?"

I take out my phone and pull up a picture of Butters. She's in the bathtub, lathered with shampoo. I combed the fleas from her fur for forty-five minutes the day I rescued her. They came off in clumps like tiny landslides.

"She's cute," says my dad.

"Yeah, she was a stray."

"Where's Seth tonight?"

SETH INVITED ME to Black Box the night before. I came in at the end of a demonstration by a local experimental dancer. She was a middle-aged woman with olive skin and close-cut hair, dressed in a black linen midriff two-piece, shoeless on the smooth concrete of the gallery's floor. She practiced a kind of dance involving spelling with her body, and explained how the sound of a name is inherently linked to a precise lexicographical gesture, which she demonstrated with names from the audience. People were seated on risers. I recognized many of them as self-proclaimed "art workers," owning property downtown or otherwise working in the nonprofit sector. The dancer assumed the position of an egg, on her knees, bent over herself. I stood near the back, in the aisle. The first notes of Janis Joplin's "Little Girl Blue" came down from the ceiling, and the lonely guitar crept through muted darkness. The dancer broke open, like a flower blooming underwater.

After, Seth closed the gallery but left the risers up with the folding chairs on them. He extracted a tripod screen and projector from the closet where he keeps the mop, and cued up Peter Greenaway's *A Zed & Two Noughts*. In it the wives of zoologist brothers die in a swan-induced car crash, and the men become obsessed with rotting. Paolo had suggested it. Paolo will be finishing his MFA in studio art in New York just as we're arriving. Seth talks about him like he's Jesus.

Seth visited Paolo last month while deciding whether or not to move with me to the city. For the first time, he sent me long, rambling love letters via email. The first came as I was finishing a twelve-hour shift at the Pizza Shack. *You didn't know I had noticed you pacing the halls of our high school like some animal in a cage,* he said. I read it standing with one hand on the oven door. *After you left for New York, I remember thinking of you from that great distance. I would try to remember what you looked like. I would conjure you in my mind, recall the shift in contrast between your freckles and your pale skin.*

I walked home greasy and floating at three in the morning. I knew for the first time with certainty that he loved me. I read his emails over and over. *I'd see your pale green eyes, forever piercing my thoughts.*

A swan, a car crash, a woman maimed. Seth held my hand through the movie. He crept from my wrist to the waistband of my jeans. We saw a long, still, accelerated shot of a zebra decomposing.

Afterward, we stacked chairs and carried the risers to the shed in the alley. It was a thick, wet night, with fireworks going off over the bay. A storm was lowering, cool and heavy.

Most of Seth's time is spent at Black Box, but most of his income comes from his part-time job at a kava bar on Sunset Beach. He has to be there at six in the morning. "I can't stay, but I'll walk you home," he said.

HIS EMAILS CAME every day he was gone, each one longer and more embroidered. *It began to rain,* he wrote on the last day. We hadn't talked on the phone for the duration of his trip; he hated talking on the phone. Instead, I'd imagine him sitting at a coffee shop, perhaps somewhere near Union Square, spending an hour or more of each evening distilling what he'd taken in since the last time he'd written to me. The sun falling over the wooden tables. Through the tall, clear windows, light spilling over a yellowing wall of magazines. I imagined him imagining me receiving him, taking his words into my corneas. *I thought I could walk a straight line through Central Park, but I ended up walking a parabola from 85th to 80th,* he said. *I became disoriented while trying to return.* Each line held metaphorical properties. *And one redeeming moment came when I had to urinate—*I pictured this; was aroused—*I turned to face west moments before the sky opened up. Suddenly fireflies lit the walkway in daytime.*

"IT'S GOING TO be a busy week," he said on our walk home from the gallery, stopping at a bench beside a retention pond. We were midway between our apartments. He wanted to talk. "You may not see me much." He had one week to finish bringing his senior thesis together to complete the BFA he's been working on for six years. "Where are you hoping we'll go?" he asked me.

I sat. "I know you need to go home."

"No, that's not what I'm asking. I'm asking, why do you want me to move with you?"

"Why do you want to come?"

"I don't know, Nina. I think New York has something to offer me, but it will also steal a part of my sanity. I have a community here. I have a reputation."

I looked out over the standing water. Its perimeter was small and greasy, likely toxic, full of trash.

"I'm also thinking of you," he said.

"That's good."

"That's what you wanted to hear, right?"

"Yeah."

"Then, yes. I'm thinking about you."

At home, I found Butters sleeping in a basket of dirty clothes. My bedroom was a mess of boxes and stacks of books and pictures taken off the walls leaning together, their corners wrapped in bubble plastic. I lay on my bed and stared at the ceiling. Butters climbed over my chest and I held her there. Her breath smelled sickly sweet.

five

A week after the dance performance, I'm in the lobby of *The Planet*'s offices in Ybor. Brian has asked to see me. The floor is an open-style, bare-brick loft space, divided up with chic midcentury furniture and vintage cubicle walls. A neon sign above the sofa in the waiting area reads, *DON'T GO VIRAL—START AN EPIDEMIC*. This morning, I filed a story about health care for homeless people. It's possible Brian wants to talk about it. It's more likely he wants to see me for personal reasons. Since we began sleeping together six months ago, we've been doing it mostly in his car, or in public restrooms, or on the spongy floor of my termite-infested living room. Then, a few nights ago, he paid for an Uber to bring me to his house in Tampa. A blue craftsman on a brick street lined with oaks and Spanish moss; the middle-class domesticity of it surprised me. I had always thought of Brian as a boy, not as a man—a few years my senior, in his early thirties but by no means paying a mortgage or mowing a lawn. The stability of his living situation placed him in a higher category. I climbed a set of wooden steps to a shady porch with hanging plants and a red-painted door. The Velvet Underground's "Pale Blue Eyes" played inside the house. I looked down at my rolled-up cutoffs and V-neck and dirty black Converse, feeling underdressed.

Brian answered the door with a camera in his hand. It was expensive-looking. I guessed it was the one he had used to take the soft-focus pictures of his ex I'd seen on Instagram a month ago, just before they broke up. He had confided in me about his grief, and I wanted to be compassionate as he mourned the loss of their future. I vaguely wondered if his confidences were strategic, meant to draw me in, to show me how vulnerable he could be, but I fell for it anyway. I swiped through the photo set compulsively: Erin with her daughters, Erin laughing, Erin sleeping on a beach towel. Long after I stopped swiping, I still saw images of Erin projected onto the screen of my mind.

"Stand still," he said, and aimed the lens at my face. Though I had imagined this moment, it was disappointing to see it enacted, his seduction requiring a prop. Inside the house was painted with accent walls of lime and blueberry. A large, flat-screen TV was mounted in the living room of leather L-couches and a chrome-legged coffee table. It was very IKEA. The few personal touches were black-and-white still lifes and obvious band posters, Wilco and Bowie.

He fumbled with the button of my shorts. We stumbled past the entrance to the eat-in kitchen, and he pinned me against the door frame of his bedroom and fingered me until wetness ran down my legs. "Lie down," he said, and I noticed then that his room was empty. It was as if he'd just moved in. No dresser, no curtains hung on the windows, an open closet with a few collared shirts. Suddenly I felt cold, but I still crossed the room obediently to a mattress dressed in white sheets on the bamboo floor. I was sparking at the illicit feel of the setting, like amateur porn. Brian followed behind me and cupped my breasts in his hands. He circled my nipples. I pulled my shirt over my head and unhooked my bra. I turned around to face him.

"You shaved for me," he said, and knelt on the mattress. He swept his fingers over my vulva. He pushed me back and climbed onto my chest. He was still fully clothed. I sucked him until he was almost cumming; then he turned me over and laid me on my stomach. He teased me. He lifted my hips in his hands. "Does your boyfriend fuck you like this?"

WE LAY BREATHING. The sheets were undone from the corners. I was dizzy with confusion, shame, seduction, exertion, as if Brian had drugged me. "Do you like being with me?" he asked into my hair.

"Yes," I said.

He kissed my ear. "I feel like we're good companions."

We were sticky, my ass nestled in his lap as he held me around the middle. I felt his dick going flaccid and was moved by the tenderness this inspired. We hadn't had time to use a condom, so when I adjusted myself, his cum leaked out of me.

"I don't want you to talk about my boyfriend," I said.

HE'S TOLD ME he has an hour-long lunch break. To kill time while I wait for him, I read a craft book that includes a short story at the conclusion of each chapter. The chapter on imagery concludes with Alice Munro's "Wild Swans," which strikes me as a naughty choice for an academic text. I take a picture of the paragraph of the inexperienced teenager orgasming for the first time. She's assisted or forced by the minister sitting next to her on the train. A flock of swans takes flight all at once from the wet field streaking past her window. I text the photo to Brian. A minute later, he's standing over me. "Want to go for a walk?" he says.

He checks his phone in the elevator and glances around the lobby when the doors open, as if someone may be waiting for him there. He guides me by the shoulder out of the building, and it occurs to me that he may be trying to hide me. We turn onto the main strip and aim ourselves at a block of restaurants with wrought-iron balconies. I assume he's taking me to the Japanese bistro with high booths where we usually go for the Love Boat special. "I met someone you know," I say as we pass a hookah bar full of teenagers. "You worked for her father."

He's quiet. He takes a napkin out of his pocket and wipes his nose, as if to redirect a feeling. The girl is our new hostess at the Pizza Shack. She's nineteen and according to her was fourteen when she met Brian, fifteen when they began sleeping together. Brian was twenty-eight, and the events manager at her father's bookstore. They'd talk about writing while she put in shifts after school, shelving books. He read some of her early poems—then he began leaving poems in her backpack, to be found when she was alone. On the day her father fired him, Brian stood in the parking lot, screaming at him: "She's the second woman I've ever loved!"

The girl was hired at the Pizza Shack two weeks ago, but because I work in the kitchen, and she's in front, I hadn't met her until yesterday. She happened to be cleaning silverware when I refilled one of my two complimentary drinks per shift. "I don't always work here," I'd told her, though she hadn't asked me. "I'm actually a writer." She asked if I was published. I said I write for *The Planet*.

Then she said, "Do you know Brian Beasley?"

"So you work together now?" he says.

"Sometimes," I say.

He nods. He looks away from me into a storefront where an old Cuban man sits rolling cigars. "Did she tell you we dated?" he says.

"Something like that."

"Her father didn't support it."

"She's a lot younger than you are."

"I don't really think that matters, though, do you?" He stops abruptly. His expression implies that he's said something radical. He turns away from me again and steps into the darkness of the cigar shop, covering his face. The Cuban man in the window has stopped rolling to watch him. He bends at the waist. I step inside as well and rub his back. He dries his eyes on his sleeve.

"I'm sorry," he says.

"Don't be."

"It's been an emotional day."

"I shouldn't have brought it up."

"I was never sure what I even meant to her," he says. "She was the first person I ever truly loved."

We walk to the bistro. It's empty and intensely air-conditioned, with club music turned down low. They seat us in a round booth large enough for four people, and we slide in on opposite sides. Brian orders two beers. I order water.

"There's something I need to talk to you about," he says. I expect him to finish the story of my new coworker. "My mother is ill."

"I'm so sorry."

"I don't really talk about this with many people. She's been sick for a long time. She has a disease that attacks her brain."

He stares at the center of the table. I watch his attention shift from the wood grain to his memory. I watch him try to wrap his mind around an enormous truth. "It's genetic and incurable. I talked to her on the phone today and I'm going to see her this fall, in New York."

I take his hand. I wish I had a mother with an incurable disease. Then I could value spending time with her while she was alive. I'd have the luxury of avoiding her if her suffering overwhelmed me. I could wager that she would still be there for me, at least emotionally, when I figured out how not to be a coward. I would have time to make peace with her before she died.

"Listen," he says. His eyes are bloodshot. "There's a chance I may have it, but they won't even test you for it unless they know you're not going to kill yourself."

"But how can you know that?"

"They interview you."

The drinks arrive. Brian orders the Love Boat. He slides closer to me and rests his hand on my thigh. He kisses me, and his tongue is aggressive, forcing its way into my mouth. I kiss him back, out of politeness.

"I'd need to prove that I have someone who's not going to leave me if I'm diagnosed," he says. "It doesn't have to be a wife. It can be a sister, or a girlfriend, or a best friend. A stable, long-term relationship. Like I thought I'd have with Erin." He rubs my leg. "Nina, I'm wondering if you can be that person."

The sushi chef is watching us through the glass. I see him preparing our special. I say yes, and we both know that I'm lying. It's what he wants to hear, and there's nothing else I can say: he needs the lie to sustain him. The knife is slicing, and the chef lowers his eyes to lift a pad of fish onto the rice. Brian holds me and cries into my shirt. I tell him I love him. I try to mean it.

A nd then he said, 'This is my attempt to lay a foundation, Nina. You need to address your male-domination insecurities—'"

"Wait a minute—"

"'—and balance your acutely sophisticated psychological level of awareness with your feminine sexual identity.'"

"I don't understand," says Odessa.

I shake my head.

"Stop trying to decode it," says Claudette.

"Do I have male-domination insecurities?" I ask, leaning over the truck console. There are a few hours of daylight left, so Odessa and I are taking Claudette to the beach. She's been isolating since learning that Jared is fucking Sofia, her best friend from private school.

"Does he mean that I'm paranoid of being dominated, or simply that I'm insouciant?"

"He means that his ego is fragile," says Odessa. She ashes out the window and pulls her sunglasses down on her face. We go over a causeway, and the sun opens up over the ocean; we lower onto the barrier islands, and it disappears behind a row of pastel-colored luxury hotels.

"But I wasn't attacking his ego."

"You were emailing another dude."

"He's a contributor to *Numina*."

"How do you know him?" says Claudette.

"We went to college together."

They nod. I pack the dugout and pass it to Claudette. "Seth is a mongoloid," says Odessa, parking in the dirt lot of a tiki bar. "And he's petty. This is not what he's upset about, and I know you know what I'm talking about." We walk to the covered patio at the to-go window and wait for margaritas. *Pet Sounds* plays over the speakers. It's the album that was playing in Seth's father's portable CD player when the truck hit him, the only thing that remained intact.

The county posted a red tide update this morning saying conditions were clear at Treasure Island, but the bloom is spreading like a bloodstain, and from here the water appears brownish. They've hauled thousands of dead animals off the beaches each week since the infection began. We promised Claudette that if we couldn't lie on the sand, we'd get drunk. We'll get drunk either way.

"He needs to come get his shit," says Claudette. I knew this was coming. "It's disrespectful. Moe could have asked anyone."

Seth's senior show for his six-year BFA was supposed to be held at Madre's, the coffee shop where Jared and Claudette work. The shop's artwork rotates once a month, and Moe, the owner, invited Seth to be the featured artist, but Seth is a chronic procrastinator. He's constantly occupied, but when it comes to making work on a deadline, he can't do it. At the last minute, unable to finish the paintings for his senior show, he decided instead to hang his "archive" at Madre's "as a mixed-media installation querying the basis for painting."

On the day he was supposed to hang his show, he arrived at the coffee shop with three Tupperware storage bins full of what any layman would consider trash—discarded takeout menus, prayer tracts, cardboard signs asking for change—to which he'd attached some abstract personal significance. He'd collected these items over a decade of "unconscious curation": in other words, if he'd wanted to pick something up from the gutter, he had. Only later did he think about why. By the act of taking them all in together at once, viewers would be asked to glean the specific lens through which Seth viewed them, both at the time of their collection, or "connotatively," and also "denotatively," as a set. Or they could simply appreciate their surfaces: the marks of car tires, the historical weight of a discarded La Luz tour poster.

He opened a box of T-pins and commenced hanging these items on the wall of Madre's. He'd completed half of one wall by closing time. He's now halfway through his month as the featured artist and still he hasn't completed the installation, nor acknowledged Moe's attempts to reach him. The walls of Madre's are full of holes. I've tried bringing it up with him, but he refuses to discuss it with me, and now, because I "insisted" on talking about it, he's barely speaking to me. The last time I saw him, he blew up at me, attacking my character, basically calling me feral.

"It's disrespectful," says Claudette. "We have hundreds of customers every day."

"Did Seth really think someone would want to buy a kid's homework he found in the garbage?"

"He could have just said, 'I need more time, maybe later in the year.'"

"He won't even text me back now."

They look at me.

"It's about supporting local artists. I thought Seth believed in that," says Odessa.

We find a place on the sand. We ignore the people coughing

around us: the telltale scratch of red tide on the back of the throat, the essence beneath the salt on the air, mingling with sunscreen.

"It just looks irresponsible and shitty."

"It's entitled."

"It's embarrassing for Moe."

"Will you just shut the fuck up, please?" I'm standing with our umbrella open behind me. It's bright red with the sun coming through it.

"At the very least, he could apologize," says Claudette.

"Am I Seth?"

"He'll never do that," says Odessa.

"No, he'll ghost you."

I walk away. I point myself at a mass grave of decomposing fish. I sit in the water and watch some teenagers make out while I tell my pelvic muscles to let me pee. A dead jelly the size of a dinner plate floats past me, translucent with a cross-section of dense tissue in its center. I visualize a water balloon untied and turned upside down, a broken egg yolk. I sit in a pool of my own waste.

When I return, they're talking about Claudette's continued inability to orgasm. She was raised Southern Baptist, and Jared is only the third person she's slept with. It sometimes makes me scared for her. "I've reached the point now where I don't care if it happens," she says. "It shouldn't be a conquest." She reaches into her backpack and digs out a copy of *Women Who Run with the Wolves*. She covers her face in sunscreen. We rest our heads on rolled-up towels. "I could always tell Jared was trying to do it. It was too much pressure."

"You need to learn to get yourself off first," says Odessa.

"Masturbation has just always freaked me out."

"Watch some porn," I say.

"Porn makes me feel disgusting."

I FALL ASLEEP for a few hours. When I come to, the sun has shrunk near the horizon and everyone on the beach has been replaced with a new person. A family is making hot dogs on a camp grill a few feet away. On our other side, a group of frat boys is openly smoking a blunt, listening to the local reggaeton station. I light a cigarette. My mouth feels pasty after I take a drag, and I reach for our bottle of water. It's been heating while we slept and I enjoy the plastic after-taste. I consider that maybe the men at the tiki bar who always buy us drinks will leave us alone if we tell them we're lesbians, but then again they might not. Odessa is sleeping on her side with a balled shirt over her face. I rest my hand on her bicep. "There's karaoke," I say. She pulls the shirt down. We listen to the tiki bar. "Yeah," she says. I hold the water in front of her face. She pushes it away.

The sign on the chalkboard above the bar reads *Attitude Adjustment Hour,* with a list of specials underneath. I mark our territory with an ashtray. We rehydrate with several Long Island iced teas. There's a long-haired hippie on the microphone singing Creedence Clearwater Revival when Odessa leans into me and says, "Ian is out on parole." She has a permanent restraining order against Max's father. He's a year younger than us and has been in prison for the last five years. "He's doing better," she says. "He's working at the garden store on MLK."

"Be careful," I say. By the time Ian went to prison, I was living in New York, so I didn't see the worst of it. When I did come home, I rarely saw Ian. Odessa and Max were living with him in his mother's house at the time, a mansion on Tierra Verde. I'd run into him downtown getting drunk alone, or picking fights with other dudes at Crowbar. I'd been getting drunk with Ian since we were teenagers, but in those last few years, he began to scare me.

"I invited him here," says Odessa.

"When, just now?"

"I want you to see him."

They call our names at the microphone. Odessa hangs back at the bar to watch as Claudette and I wait for the opening bars of "Magic Man" to play. We sing about love cast over us like a spell, how the failed attempts of other women to save us from going under haunt us in the end. We hold each other through the chorus. I have the distinct feeling of Odessa slipping away from me, and when I open my eyes, there is Ian standing by her at our ashtray. His hair is black like a wolverine, but trimmed, clean-cut around the ears. He watches us, rubbing Odessa's shoulders.

"Don't leave me," she says when I return to her.

"Okay, baby, I won't," I say.

I hug her and feel in her embrace that she's performing for Ian.

"So why are you?" she says, pouting. I pull away from her, and her eyes are blue and wet, and I look into them for the real reason she's saying this, what she's actually telling me she's afraid of.

"You don't even appreciate what you have," she says. "You're very privileged, Nina."

Ian gives her some water. He stands over her, staring at me, and I weakly hand her a napkin.

"I work really hard," I say.

"Yeah, I know," she says, wiping her nose. "I didn't say you don't work hard. I work harder than you do."

I feel Ian's arm brush against mine as he sits, and his knee presses into me. He takes Odessa's hand. "I don't even get a hello?" he says.

"Hey, Ian," I say. "Odessa, I'm sorry."

She lights a Parliament. I watch her smoke and I turn to Ian. He reaches up and roughly massages my neck.

"Thanks for being supportive," he says.

When he goes to the bathroom, she says, "He's been staying over every night. I'm waiting tables and dancing, and he stays with Max. I have no time for myself, and I can't rely on my mother anymore. All I want is some help. I want to create. I want to turn our garage into a studio. I just want some space for myself. I hope he's ready to be a man, to be a father."

I'm hungover at the hypnotist's the next morning. The news is on in her waiting room. I view this as an oversight on her part—she should have known I would find it distressing. I watch and drink freezing water from the cooler. Flint is still toxic. Ebola is spreading to neighboring countries. A frustrated virgin in California killed six people before shooting himself. Children seeking asylum from one dictatorship are falling into the hands of another. Everything that enters our bodies is poisonous.

In her office I beg the hypnotist to help me. I tell her that I harbor a lot of anger. I often feel overstimulated and have the urge to flee, and she tells me that my fight-or-flight response is disregulated. "Let's try some grounding exercises," she says. I identify all the red items in my vicinity—a pillow, a candle—then touch and verbally identify objects—a rock garden, a small fountain. This helps a little. She tips me back on the recliner and asks me to close my eyes and stand inside an early memory of fear.

"How old are you?" she asks.

"Seven."

"Imagine the scene in detail."

I'm standing at the top of my street at dawn. I'm wearing a gum-colored backpack stuffed with a shirt, a pair of shorts, and seventeen dollars of allowance savings. I'm waiting for Odessa, who lives on the next street, because we're going to run away together. It was her idea, and I agreed because I saw that she needed me and there was no saying no to her, to her desperation.

Neither of us can tell time, or maybe she forgets about me, or gets caught sneaking out, or changes her mind. I wait as the day grows hot. No one comes outside to check on me. I have no plan for where I'm going. I haven't thought beyond this moment.

My father's car appears beside me. It's cherry-colored. He pauses at the stop sign, turns left, and drives on. I see his profile through the window, opaque, fixed in a forward position. He disappears around the corner of the first cross-street.

I kneel on the sidewalk and disrupt an anthill to observe it. A fire ant climbs onto my thumb and the burn of its pincers feels distant, but my fury grows hotter the longer I wait for my mother to find me. The ant pierces my skin again and I crush it.

The hypnotist tells me to kneel and place my arm around the shoulders of my inner child. I do. I remind my inner child that the world is not a safe place because of other people, and I turn her to face down the street in the direction of our house, with its familiar curve of sidewalk. I remind her that she doesn't know how to cook, spell, or ask for help.

For the next week, my inner child observes the ant bite turn carmine and harden with pus. She finds that she enjoys the sting of touching it lightly from time to time. She breaks it open with a needle and watches the fluid, yellow and bloody, flow over her wrist. She peels the scab each day until it's pink. Over time it turns into a bright, puckered scar.

THE NIGHT BEFORE I'm to leave for New York, Seth breaks his punishment of silence and taps on my window. It's a gentle tapping, unsure if it wants to be heard, and when I open the side door, he's standing there with his messenger bag slung across his body, letting it ride high like some kind of emo hipster. I'm met with a memory of seeing him at a Saves the Day concert in high school. He was crying and singing along with the lyrics, even then equating pain with love.

"I know I've been holding you responsible for things that are more often than not my own projections," he says.

"Thanks for saying that."

"May I come inside?"

He stands in the center of my living room, empty other than twenty or so boxes of books since I hauled most of my furniture to the alley. "I'd still like to come to New York," he says. I note that he doesn't say he wants to come *with me.* "You understand that it's hard for me to trust people. My parents divorced and my father died soon after. It's affected me in ways even I don't fully comprehend."

"Consider therapy."

"I have."

The anger I feel is minor compared to the terror that engulfs me when I realize that Seth anchors me in the world. He's like a cell phone or my keys. His life provides a groove along which mine can travel. In New York, I could get lost, be kidnapped, die and be found in a river, and there would be no one around to claim my body—it happens all the time. There are germs as big as rats, men pressing against you in the turnstile, milky brown lakes of oily rain. Seth sees the anguish in my eyes and forces me to bribe him for protection, knowing I find it degrading to admit to having needs. He drags his feet to remind me—or himself—that he has the option to go alone. He doesn't need me; might prefer not to have me. The space between us reveals my desire for him, as I am always the one trying to bridge it.

He kneels to say hello to Butters. He lays his hands on her very biblically. "Nina," he says, "she looks weak."

I've failed to notice how Butters's appearance has changed in the last days. I've been too distracted with the drama and disarray of moving. A month ago, Butters was eating three tuna Fancy Feasts a day, licking the sides of the cans. Now she smells like my nana's medicine cabinet. I haven't fed her tonight because she still hasn't touched her food from this morning.

Taking a cat to the doctor wasn't a practice while I was growing up, either with Skittles, our indoor cat, or Nugget, our outdoor cat. Until she wasn't, Skittles was healthy; we knew just by looking at her; she was a cat, a simple creature. To complicate her by suggesting that she might need a checkup was ludicrous. "Don't be hysterical," my father would say. This was before every cutlet had a name and an origin story. I never learned how one even goes about taking a cat to the doctor. How much would they charge me? What should I tell them about the cat's condition; what do I know? What have I honestly observed? Her bowel movements? Her water intake? Her affect? Were cats not solely for pleasure?

I remember standing in the street with my parents as a child, laughing at the humorous misspelling of a note in bubbly, feminine handwriting, taped to our mailbox: *FEED YOU CAT*. There was a mild cringe in the background, which I now recognize as guilt. Of course we fed Nugget. Did we leave her food on the porch to get rained on? Sure. Were there old pellets and bugs in it? Yes. Was she ever allowed inside the house? No, but my parents assured me she didn't want to be in the house.

We don't know what happened to Nugget. We moved and set her outside in our new neighborhood, and never saw her again. My parents weren't concerned. We never put up signs with her picture on them. "She probably tried to go home," said my father. But our old home was miles away, and I knew she wouldn't find it. She would never find her way back from it, even if she did. She would have to cross back over the freeway, if she made it across the first time.

"I think we should take her to your father's house," Seth says. He holds Butters like the *Pietà*. "I'll drive us there."

My father makes her a bed with towels on the floor of the bathroom. For some reason, this makes sense to all of us. It also seems natural to assume that, given our timeline, given our inability to care for Butters in that moment, given our move, financially and emotionally, my father will take over her care.

"She's very ill," Seth says, stroking her on the floor of my father's bathroom. She sits on all fours with her tummy hovering above the tile. She's wasted away in the course of a day, like something vampiric has taken possession, sucking the life from her.

Seth asks me if I would like to say goodbye to her. I say no. I sit with her for a moment on the tile, but her scent and her suffering are too potent. Her eyes plead for something I can't give her, have failed to give her. I stand to leave the bathroom, with Seth's eyes following me, judging.

THE NEXT MORNING, we wake together in my father's condo. Butters is still alive. It's implicit that my father will take her to the doctor. When Seth and I arrive at his apartment with the moving van, he has packed nothing: not his art supplies, his hundreds of records, his dozens of ironic thrift store shirts, his chaise longue, or the archives. A few times, in moments of panic, in weeks past, I've alluded to the immanency of our move, have offered to help him with packing, but he is avoidant, ashamed to be stalling under deadline. The word "stress" passes through his lips twice a day like he's chewing on it: "I'm so *shtreshed*," he says, touching his forehead, where the stress is located, in his brain.

Now he's crouched over a box of old photographs. I come up behind and see him admiring one from his fifth birthday. He appears to be staring into an area of damage in the collodion. "We need to go," I say. "I'm throwing this trash bag away." I slam the door to the outside stairs.

On the street, my mother is leaning against our moving van. I didn't invite her, haven't talked to her in three years. My father must have told her where to find me. She's wearing a T-shirt with the neck cut out, a hot-pink bathing suit, and a pair of cargo shorts. Her skin is the color of bronzer. Her hair is cut short.

The last time we spoke, I told her, "I think I'm in love." It was just after I'd met Seth. I was sitting on the stoop of my apartment, away from Mission. The orchid tree across the street was blooming, and lavender and fuchsia littered the lawn. "Of course you are," she said. "Falling in love is your favorite thing to do." She said I was codependent and couldn't be alone. That she wouldn't come to see me as long as Seth and I were together. She couldn't pretend to approve, and I needed to be focusing on sobriety and school, not other people. It was then that I told her I wouldn't be going back. I said it to be spiteful, but I wondered whether I meant it. I briefly considered running away with Mission to hop freight trains.

"I know you don't want me here," she says. "I just wondered if I could talk to you for one minute."

An unkind person would say no. I walk with her to her graphite SUV. It's already cool inside when we climb in. She blasts the air-conditioning, and I angle it away from my face.

"I need to tell you something about your uncle Bruce," she says.

I expect her to tell me he's dead, which wouldn't be bad. He's a raging alcoholic after working in the sex crimes unit for thirty years. "He was inappropriate with me when we were children. It went on through grade school," she says. "I've been living with a lot of resentment and pain. Shame. My actions toward you and everyone have been terrible. The last time we talked, I had a revelation afterward, and looked back at the whole history of hurting you. I can't believe what I said to you. It's not right, Nina. I'm not right. I'm sorry."

I look at her and can tell she's not lying, as she never apologizes. Uncle Bruce was never seen at Christmas. I ask her if Jude and my father know about it, and she says yes. My uncle Jude saw it happen. He couldn't stop it. He was a child. My pop-pop and nana knew, too, but chose to ignore it. Children experiment, said my nana. "She told me not to disgrace my brother."

Seth comes up to the window. He's carrying boxes stacked in front of his face. I tell my mother I need to help him. I say we'll talk later. I open the car door onto the realization that my mother needs me to hold space for her so that she can forgive herself, that this task has fallen to me. "I love you," she says, and I say I love her, too. She's suffering; I'm not a sociopath. I'm in pain. We all are.

eight

In New York our mattress sits atop another, atop a box spring. The basement we were told we could use for storage is padlocked, and our furniture and other worldly belongings are Tetris-ed into our below-street-level, furnished, East Williamsburg Airbnb studio sublet. We're unable to open boxes, so although our belongings are close around us, they are inaccessible. The unit is a single room with a bathroom divided off from the kitchen by a plastic hospital-blue curtain. There are two small windows above eye level. We're lit from above by a bare bulb suspended on a cord hanging from the low ceiling. When Seth shits, I smell it. When we argue, the neighbors hear us. I fall asleep next to him while he watches *Antichrist* on his laptop in our bed. I wake to Charlotte Gainsbourg circumcising herself with hedge shears. I ask him to turn it off. There is nowhere for me to go when he refuses.

He's desultory, grumpy, and blameful for what he perceives as my failure to house us properly. For weeks prior to the move, I sent him listings. "I did not spend any time in front of my computer today," he'd say when I asked what he thought of them.

I find myself missing Brian. As if he felt me crossing the line into Georgia, he texted me a line from "Pale Blue Eyes." I was touched he remembered which song was playing when he answered the door my first time at his house. I responded with the next line.

Since then, I've felt inspired to send him dispatches on the Hare Krishnas in Union Square, the bleeding man on the J train, one-eyed bodega cats, borderline-contaminated street meat, Hasidic men in vans, topless book clubs in Central Park, the man in Atlantic Terminal playing "Ave Maria" on repeat on a beat-up, child-sized violin. I want to bring Brian close to me, or bring me close to him, but more than that, I've found, seeing New York as a collection of details to notice and send to Brian brings me into closer contact with my city of residence. Brian is an outlet, recipient, and depository of my observations as a native returning from exile. He is my audience, and I want to entertain, educate, enlighten, intrigue, and arouse him.

SETH IS SLEEPING when I get home. He was also sleeping when I left five hours ago. I study his face for signs of consciousness. I set my laptop at his feet with the camera facing away from him, at chest level on the double-high mattress. I stand on a chair and mute the speakers, and the Photo Booth timer counts to three. The screen flashes and produces a thumbnail of my ass. The camera counts again and snaps a thumbnail of my tits. I wet my mouth and lean forward. It counts again, and I slide two fingers inside myself. I send the images to Brian. I delete them from the roll. Seth sleeps.

When he wakes an hour later, we walk to Trophy Bar, beneath the M train. We're here to celebrate that I've been offered a job as the personal assistant to the *New York Times* bestselling author of what is popularly known as the Jewish *DaVinci Code*. Part of my compensation for assisting him will be twenty-four-hour access to his office in Midtown, which makes it feel as if I have my own studio.

We bring our happy hour IPAs to the outdoor patio with no breeze. "What did you do today?" I ask Seth. I'm hoping he'll tell me he looked for a job, since we're also looking for a real apartment.

"I went for a walk with Paolo," he says. "He asked me if I would help him paint a mural he's been hired to complete."

"What's he painting?"

"The client has asked for something tropical that may include animals."

"Can I see it?"

"That may be hard. It's in a private home."

"Whose?"

"A couple who is having their first child."

My phone vibrates in my purse. I reach inside and tilt it in my hand to read the message on the lock screen privately. Next time send a video.

You first, I say. I turn it facedown. It vibrates again.

"When are you starting?"

"We'll meet in the space this weekend to measure and do sketches."

"How much are they paying you?"

"They're not paying me. They're paying Paolo."

"How much are they paying Paolo?"

"I haven't asked him."

It vibrates again. I glance at the screen. You have to wait for it.

"How much is Paolo paying you?"

"Paolo pays me in friendship. He is a good friend to have here."

"I see."

"This is the gift economy of art, Nina."

THE THRILLER WRITER subleases a corner office on the tenth floor of a skyscraper near Grand Central. My cubicle is visible through his glass wall. I feel him watching me as I carry out his various assignments. I offload photos from his family vacation, upload them to Google Play, and share them with his elderly father in Boca Raton. I book his travel arrangements to Jewish Community Centers. I post factoids related to the content of his book on his Facebook author page. He pays me twenty-five dollars an hour, but only for those hours when I'm actively working for him at my desk. He doesn't pay me for the hours during which I'm not working, even if I'm sitting at my desk. I have to sit at my desk all day, whether or not I'm working for him. When I'm not working for him, it's understood that I do my own writing. I keep a time sheet, which I submit at the end of each week for us to go over together. He asks me to explain my logged hours, then cuts me a personal check. He gives me his leftover kosher sandwiches out of pity. I accept them because I was taught that it's rude to turn down food.

I rack up billable hours trying to stomach his bestseller. Though it was published with a major press, it reads as if it's never come within ten yards of an editor. It's riddled with inconsistencies, plot holes, bad grammar. It's also five hundred pages long. He's asked me to comb through it and make suggestions for linking it to the next book in the series, which he hasn't yet begun. When he sees me reading at my desk, he comes out of his office. "What are you doing?" he asks. He says that reading is recreational, not billable work, and that I should do it outside the office. The thriller writer believes my investment in his writing is equal to my investment in my own, that I should be happy to read his novel on my own time, that I should not consider reading this garbage labor. He adds that no one wears bare legs in Midtown; that I'm to wear stockings to work from now on.

His office is housed in his friend's insurance company. I don't know anyone's name, and no one seems to understand why I'm here. I watch them all leave at six o'clock while I stay to work on the novel I abandoned around the time I started dating Seth. I'm rewriting the first two chapters. My unnamed protagonist has just met the person she'll eventually have sex with at a college party in front of everyone. I'm trying to articulate what's so attractive about him, or at least what would attract my protagonist to him. He seems brooding from a distance but up close is humble, with a darkness that calls to hers. The question is: What is the nature of my protagonist's darkness?

When I can't write anymore, I begin to compose a letter to Brian. Over the ensuing month, I've felt increasingly like what I have with him is love. I send him movie stubs stapled to NYC postcards, haikus scrawled on greasy dollar-pizza bags, used books I buy on the street. Right now, I'm writing an account of my day. I craft detailed descriptions of teen crust punks selling stolen bottles of 5-hour Energy. I tell him how lonely it is to be new again here. I know he'll understand. I tell him I look forward to seeing him in the fall when he comes to visit his mother in Bay Ridge, Brooklyn. I ask him about his mother, how she's feeling. I tell him to give her my love.

I include the thriller writer's office as a return address. I imagine this igniting a longing to use it. I imagine Brian tucking my letter into a carved wooden cigar box designated for the preservation of my memory. I use the company postage machine and drop the letter into the Outgoing Mail bin.

I'M WALKING HOME from my first independent writing workshop. My MFA program begins in six weeks, and I want to be prepared to handle criticism. My class meets weekly at the Le Pain Quotidien on Bryant Park. It's part of an unschool series that markets itself as a more affordable, democratic, sustainable, and life-affirming alternative to the MFA. My instructor is a year younger than I am, and out as a lesbian, but all of the characters in her novel are straight. Her teaching philosophy centers on the belief that we can best serve each other by asking questions, and that the holiest question is "How?" Five of my seven classmates are old enough to be my parents. I carry in my backpack seven marked-up copies of a new story from the Ira Cycle, which they have just deemed unreadable. Their questions replay in my mind. "How can Liz expect anything from Billy?" "How can she hide this from Ira?" "How can she call this a relationship?"

I call Brian. Bed-Stuy is deserted, and for the next long block, there are only warehouses with locked retracting doors displaying flyers for Black Lives Matter groups, community garden meetings, and daycares. We decided to look at this neighborhood after seeing a story in the *New York Times* suggesting it might be more affordable than some other trendy Brooklyn neighborhoods. The title of the article was "Bedford-Stuyvesant: Diverse and Changing." Using the combination of my student loans, my father's signature, Seth's new job at Dick Blick, and Paolo's brother as a roommate, we've been able to secure a two-bedroom, fourth-floor walk-up on Marcus Garvey Boulevard.

We're the only white people on our block. The day before we signed the lease, Michael Brown was shot to death in Ferguson, Missouri, and that city erupted. A month ago, cops on Staten Island choked Eric Garner until he died begging for air. We've seen the way our new neighbors look at us. Among ourselves, we refer to this as "awkward."

"Hey, it's me," I say to Brian's voicemail, scanning the street for other humans. "I thought I might catch you." I hit pound. I listen to the electronic recording. I press three to continue speaking. "Haven't talked to you in a while. I hope you're well. I had my first workshop tonight, for the story I emailed you a few days ago. Not sure if you've had a chance to read it. The workshop was really helpful. You know, I'm always here if you need to talk. Okay, hugs."

I listen to the message in its entirety and hate myself. I reflect on the possible reasons Brian has never acknowledged my snail mail. Maybe it makes him too sad to miss me. Maybe he's jealous of my deepening commitment to Seth, as we are now living together. Maybe he prefers the distant intimacy of silent connection. When I moved to New York, we hadn't taken the step of defining our relationship. It seemed to defy definitions. When I text him now, he responds, and only sometimes, hi—no emoji, no capitalization, no follow-up, no requests for nudes.

He calls me back when I'm almost home. "I'm sorry," he says, his voice raspy. "I'm sorry, Nina."

"It's okay," I say, though I don't know what he's even sorry for.

I listen to him sob for nearly a full minute. I sit on our front stoop, my heart racing. When I left for class, my downstairs neighbor was grilling on the concrete patio; now the grill is cool beneath its slip-cover. I can hear Brian put the phone down and scream. He blows his nose. He returns, still crying. He cries as he talks.

"I didn't want to tell you," he says. I stare at the concrete. "For the last two weeks, Erin and I have been talking every day. I knew she was lying to her new boyfriend, but I didn't know who her boyfriend was. She wouldn't tell me. I didn't know it was my fucking best friend."

I watch the apartment across the street. On the second floor, a small rectangle of frosted glass lights up. A figure moves near it, then away.

THE LIVING ROOM smells like weed when I enter. I notice a joint hanging in the ashtray in front of Paolo's brother, Rafael. He works for a moving company by day and moonlights as a spoken-word poet under the alias White and Woke. He sells weed and stays up all night banging on his typewriter. I've tried to relate to him as a fellow writer, but Rafael doesn't read, so the conversations don't go far. I try to loan him books, and they sit untouched on the floor of his bedroom. His bedroom is bare except for a mattress and a Tupperware bin of white T-shirts and track pants.

Leaning against the living room wall behind Rafael are Seth's in-progress paintings, close-up meditations on loose-weave textiles, in which he's taken an interest since talking with Paolo about the regrettable way Western culture has lost touch with its connection to fabric as a medium for storytelling. He paints parallel line after parallel line, then paints a perpendicular set of lines over the first set in colors both contrasting and nearly identical. He's been doing this for weeks on the same three canvases. The original lines of weave are no longer visible. They all blend together. The paint builds up.

I pass his sketchbook, beside which he's laid a sheet of my seventh grade school pictures. It was the year I cut my hair short like a boy's. I loved it at first but hated it once school started, when I had to wear it in the halls every day. Bobby Heilmann called me "GI Jane." Sensing my embarrassment, Odessa altered the hairstyle in the photos with permanent marker, leaving one untouched for comparison. Seth has reproduced the sheet in pencil in his sketchbook. On the untouched photo, he's drawn devil horns. How obvious.

"How was class?" says Rafael.

I shrug and hit the joint. "Fine, I guess. Not great." I exhale through my nose. "People don't like my protagonist."

"Why not?"

"They don't understand her."

"Does she understand herself?"

"She thinks she does, but her insight is poor."

"Have you been crying?"

"A little." I smile sadly, to elicit sympathy.

"Don't let it get to you."

I find Seth in the kitchen taking a pan of ziti out of the oven. "Who were you talking to on the steps?" he asks.

"Brian," I say without thinking. "I guess he and Erin have been talking about getting back together."

Seth doesn't respond, perhaps contemplating whether Brian is a passing curiosity. Whether I have some masturbatory compulsion to become fixated on other people. Whether, once I blow my wad on Brian, I will suddenly be disgusted with the affair, ashamed of what I'd wanted. The idea that Seth knows something about me that I don't know about myself makes him seem superior as he carries the ziti past me. I slip into the bedroom and drop my backpack and coat on the bed beside a pile of clean laundry.

"I wasn't aware you were keeping in touch with Mr. Beasley," he says from the other room.

"Oh," I say. I text Brian. **Everything will be okay. Stay strong. We'll talk over the holidays.** "A little. This is the first time we've talked on the phone."

"Interesting. I wonder why he would want to talk to you about Erin."

"Maybe he thought I could be impartial."

I return to the common area. I sit at the table and serve myself. The ziti jiggles.

"This is really good, Seth. What's in it?" says Rafael.

"Sardines," says Seth. "Can you be impartial?"

"About what?" I say, as if I've forgotten already what we were talking about. I poke a grayish mass in the center of my plate. It flakes apart. "Oh. Sure, Erin is a little grating, but I have no problem with her." I chew.

"Perhaps that's why Brian called you. Because you have no problem with her."

"I didn't ask why he called me, Seth. He was crying."

"Sounds dramatic."

"It was."

Rafael goes in for seconds. I discover that I can break the sardines up and spread them around, making them less potent.

nine

Aaron is leaning against the counter of a to-go pizza window. It's magic hour, and I'm watching him pick the bell peppers off his slice of veggie lovers' and deposit them on my plate. This is the fourth time we've hung out in two weeks. When I returned to the city, I contacted other friends from college, but the conversations all died off quickly. Except with Aaron.

His glasses slide down his nose. He pushes them back in place and fixes his hair behind his ears. A mole rides on his left cheekbone.

"My logline is 'A twenty-something runs out of money in Los Angeles and has to move back in with his parents,'" he says. His eyes are sea green and laughing. "Oh, 'And his girlfriend breaks up with him.'"

"So it's autobiographical?"

"The membrane between fiction and nonfiction is thin," he says. He places his hand on my shoulder.

"I'm not sure what you mean."

"Of course not. Nina, my golden fire, hand me a napkin. Thank you. But why even tell you this? The film will never get made."

"Don't say that."

"I'm being realistic."

"You're being a pessimist."

None of my other college friends tried to find me when I left school—only Aaron did, which was fine. I'd disappeared without telling anyone. My father encouraged me to cut ties with people who enabled my "disease."

In the harsh light of sobriety, I was embarrassed by certain choices. As the self-appointed "headmaster" of my dorm room, otherwise known as the Den of Inquiry, I had become a grotesque creature. I viewed my move back to Florida, however humiliating, as a fresh start. I could slip free of the version of myself determined by those who knew me as I was.

Three years later, Aaron showed up as a comment on an article I'd written for *The Planet,* saying, *So glad to see you writing again, Nina. I always enjoyed your stories.*

It took me a month to find the courage to respond. I remembered Aaron as the roommate of Daniel, a core participant in my former iniquity. Social media suggested Aaron was no longer friends with Daniel. It also seemed he was now an aspiring screenwriter. I emailed him asking for a script to print in *Numina.* Since then, we've exchanged emails two or three times a month.

"I need some brainstorming assistance," he says.

"Shoot."

"I need some memories to play in his head. Things to look back on fondly, but I need them to be more than just him and his girlfriend. I don't have other friends, though."

"That presents a limitation."

"Do you have any memories that I can use, as far as very brief flashbacks? You're so much better at this than I am. Things he will miss about Los Angeles. You must have had some of those as you were leaving Florida."

"Not really."

He waits.

"I had sex on the roof of a building downtown."

"Slut."

"Let me think of how I said goodbye. I sat on the seawall, smelling the Gulf. I stood for a long time in my empty apartment, appreciating the humidity of the air. I walked around my neighborhood barefoot. I ate a honeysuckle flower. I smoked a cigarette inside."

Aaron is quiet.

"Should we go?" I say. He checks the time on his phone. I'd invited Seth to see *Boogie Nights* with us at Film Forum, but I knew he would decline; he's out with Paolo, and he doesn't like Aaron. We walk to the theater and find two seats in the middle. It's otherwise empty on a Monday. Aaron leans back with his foot on the chair in front of him. I find this charmingly rude. The lights lower, and the camera pans through the opening nightclub scene. He leans over the armrest and says, "Let's make a movie together," and the darkness cloaks us and presses down. His breath is warm in my ear. He sits up again with his arm against mine.

"If we were a movie, what kind of movie would we be?" I say.

"The best film you've never seen," he says.

WE CALL OUR movie *True Love.* It follows a group of troubled, narcissistic young people as they become entangled in a series of illconceived relationships that flame out in humiliating ways. For hours each night, I sit on the floor of the locked bathroom, the only place where I can be alone in our Bed-Stuy apartment—if I close the door on the bedroom, Seth needs his phone charger, Seth needs a jacket, Seth needs his cell phone, his keys, his book, his bed. He sees that I'm irritated and accuses me of never learning to share: "It's because you're an only child," he says. I turn my back to the door. I'm Gchatting with Aaron.

I've told Seth that I'm writing and asked him to give me privacy. Through the cheap wood, I hear him crowing with Rafael, listening to Jawbreaker, banging pots in the kitchen, making dinner with dehydrated soy product he bought in bulk in Chinatown but doesn't know how to prepare.

I started to say this in the car tonight but was interrupted too many times by one thing or another and gave up, I say to Aaron. *I think the best thing to do, if we're worried about pacing, is outline.*

What I'm going to do, actually, Aaron responds, *is watch Magnolia and log everyone's screen time.*

Rafael needs to use the bathroom; I am ousted. *Brb,* I say. I quickly close the chat box and open a random Word document on my desktop. I carry my laptop, propped in the crook of my arm, demonstrating my innocence, and sit, as if in a trance, in the common area. I'm poised at the corner of the table Seth constructed from eight salvaged milk crates and an enormous piece of wood from the street. It's ugly as hell and could be infested with bedbugs, but it's multipurpose. It's our dining table, his worktable, a repository for junk mail.

"What are you writing?" says Rafael, emerging moments later, followed by a whiff of feces. The toilet is refilling, and I see a digested leaf of lettuce floating in it.

"Homework," I say.

"Already?"

"Every week."

I brush past him, back to my cave. I sit on the toilet lid with my feet on the bathtub and hit the partially smoked bowl he hides in the extra toilet paper. *Back,* I say to Aaron.

Our film doesn't have the thread that's tying everything together, he responds.

The thread is their relation to Lisa.

You're brilliant.

Or are we getting ahead of ourselves because we don't even know what everyone's story is?

There's too much potential, like diner potential, where you have too many choices on the menu and you're paralyzed, and it's also a question of, do we start really fast out the gate, and switch rapidly from character to character, then slow as the movie progresses?

And in terms of pacing, remember that some scenes will have one character, some will have four, some scenes are more significant than others (although, in a perfect story, every scene carries equal importance).

Each character's story has to be broken down into tiny segments so we can shuffle the pieces around and see what goes where, and at times it has to feel claustrophobic.

Fat legs in skinny pants, I say.

This is why we're perfect together.

You think in larger pieces, I'll fill in the details. For instance, the Buddha must feature prominently.

The Buddha resides on the dashboard of his car.

The Buddha is our mascot.

The Buddha is our protagonist.

He bought it in a flea market stall on Olvera Street, just before leaving Los Angeles. He owns nothing but the Buddha, not even his car.

The Buddha is perfect, I say.

You're perfect.

I INVITE HIM to the thriller writer's office. It's after hours, the building is dark, and I can do with it what I wish. He meets me in the lobby, and we tour the tenth floor looking for a cubicle to occupy with our story making. We pick one in a corner with greeting cards pinned to the walls and a bowl of Hershey's Kisses next to the monitor. We decide this desk belongs to Karen from accounting, and we eat her chocolates and work on *True Love*. We now maintain an almost constant stream of messages. I'm forced to carry my phone with me everywhere, as each text I send Aaron receives an immediate response. Do we take the position that Jordan is using Carissa? I say. Given her lack of experience, I think so, he says. And his obfuscation of the truth, I say. But does she really want the truth? he says. I'd want the truth, I say.

Beyond *True Love*, I've confided in Aaron about Brian, my sins, my need for a confessor. I've painted myself as a prisoner in my home, and Seth as a negligent jailer. I love him, but it's hard being with an artist, I've said. Our modes of working are totally different. Seth needs to play music while he paints, he needs to move around. I need silence. Writers are eccentric, we're private, we require a lot of personal space. But we're not always the best communicators, ironically. I think linearly. Seth thinks like a rhizome.

Sounds like my relationship with Amanda, he says. Everything came down to the way we failed to communicate.

I realize it's over now, but I never fully got closure with Brian, and while I don't want to be with him, I would like to know what happened between us from his perspective, I say. I underemphasize how I miss Brian, how I harbor intrusive fantasies of sucking him off in the shower. I say, Maybe then I could forgive myself.

Seth is an idiot. Please forgive yourself.

I'm trying.

You're doing the best you can.

Aaron can name every moon of Jupiter. He can pick up any instrument and play it by ear; he has perfect pitch. He sent me a song he recorded before leaving Los Angeles, in which he accompanies himself in four-part harmony. It's named after his favorite line from *Rain Man*. I listen to it on repeat. His voice is alto and clear like Sam

Cooke's. I memorize all of his lyrics. "I worked the lyrics over for weeks," he told me. They're full of clever lines and tell a twee love story. They're addressed to Amanda as he leaves the West Coast, before she breaks up with him two weeks later. Amanda is an actress ten years Aaron's senior. Just after he left Los Angeles, she traveled to upstate New York to shoot a movie. It was directed by the Duplass brothers, Aaron's favorite. Aaron drove up to see her and to help with the movie.

She dumped me standing in the doorway of her cabin, he said. Then we fucked in her period blood on the wood floor. It was splattering everywhere, all over us. All over the rug. She was so angry. I think she hated me.

Did you hate her? I said.

A little.

"I LOVED MOVIES when I was a kid," he tells me. Through the floor-to-ceiling windows, the moon has risen high over the Chrysler Building. I've stolen a rolling chair from the next cubicle over, and we've set our laptops side by side on Karen's desk. We sip cups of Keurig from the employee kitchen. We're lit by the glow of our screens. We've spent ten minutes writing and sixty talking. The story Aaron is telling me now is from the fifth grade. "I had plans to see *Rushmore* with my friends. Then the day before, they told me they weren't going." He unwraps a chocolate. He balls up the tinfoil and flicks it into the trash can. "Bill Murray was my favorite actor, so my mom and I went instead. Then we saw my friends at the theater," he says. He eats the chocolate.

"That's shitty," I say.

"The next day, they told me they didn't want to be my friends anymore. They said I was annoying."

I suggest including this as a subplot of *True Love*. I think I am being supportive, but he says, "I hated my childhood. It wasn't fun for me. I found it frustrating. I couldn't do anything." I'm taking notes as he talks, but he rests his hand on mine. I close my laptop, shrouding his face in darkness.

"You're not annoying," I say.

"You're sweet."

I touch a scar at the corner of his eye.

"What's this from?" I say. I trace it gently.

His lips part. He holds my gaze, and I feel his fingers wrap around my wrist. It sends a tremor up my arm. His other hand pulls my sleeve back, exposing a scar I gave myself in tenth grade.

"What's this from?" he says.

Our faces are inches apart. I smell his breath and close the distance between us. Our chairs roll together. His hand cups the back of my neck, and I climb into his lap, straddling him. My fingers lace through his hair. His other hand travels up my thigh and under my skirt.

"Come with me," I say.

But we stay there. I lean into him, grinding. He pushes my underwear to the side. I stand and drop them to the floor, sitting on Karen's desk, lifting my knees up to show him my pussy. He fingers me and I ejaculate on Karen's carpet. My cum lands in the shape of a heart. We laugh. I remember then that there's a camera in the ceiling. "Shit," I say.

I lead him to the bathroom. I wave at the motion detector and the lights come on with the fan. My body is sweating. The door swings closed behind us, and Aaron turns me and pushes me against the tile wall. It's cold against my skin. Aaron pulls my skirt above my waist.

"I love you, Nina," he says, his hand on my breast. "I'm in love with you and I think Seth doesn't deserve you."

"I love you, too, Aaron."

I climb onto the sink. I look over my shoulder and watch him in the mirror as he fucks me. I see that Aaron and I could be twins. The simple beauty of him is exhilarating. He is already close and familiar.

I'm not comfortable with you sleeping with Aaron," says my mother. I'm hiking back to the office with a box of the thriller writer's books, which I've just picked up from the Century, near Bryant Park. It's 95 degrees in the Grand Central District, and heat waves warp the sidewalk as bodies of strangers press in, close and sticky. I pause at a trash can and rest the box on it. Sharp sweetness mixes with something rotting. A homeless man is soliciting a group of tourists for change. They back away.

"I'm not sleeping with him," I say. I've communicated with my mother on a weekly basis since leaving Florida. Sometimes our exchanges are brief—cat memes, food photos—but often there are conversations requiring thirty minutes to an hour. While we talk, she browses the racks at Nordstrom's, or lays mulch for her special friend, or cleans her special friend's house, or is driving from St. Petersburg to Kissimmee because her polycule has asked her to dog-sit for them. I tell myself I'm grateful for these conversations because I love my mother and my mother needs me.

"Please explain why it's necessary," she says.

"It's not. I'm just expressing a feeling. I said that I *wanted to*."

"I think you want it for the wrong reasons. I don't think you know why you want what you want."

"What do you want?"

"It doesn't matter what I want because Dara will never give me what I want."

"Then find someone who can. Or be with yourself. What's so bad about being alone?"

"I love her. I just don't trust her family. They're not good people. Her mom is white trash, a miserable bitch. Her sister's husband is a drug dealer, and none of them respect Dara's boundaries, they all have keys to her house, they come in all the time and trash the place, and guess who cleans up after them because Dara lives like a hobo?"

"Are you sleeping together?"

"I don't like the way she touches me. I tell her how I want to be touched and how I don't want to be touched, and then she does the thing I told her not to do. Also, she smells and she's gained weight. She told me how she and her ex used to have sex, so now I have that mental picture. I'm sleeping in the bed upstairs."

"I didn't realize you were living with her."

"I have my own place, but she doesn't know about it."

"Are you going to tell her?"

"Not until I'm done furnishing it."

"So you're breaking up with her?" I prop the box on my hip and carry it farther down the block. "Mom, this sounds like a really dishonest way to go about things." I reach the thriller writer's building, and its cold air punches me in the face. I squeeze through the vestibule, nodding at the doorman, and wait for the elevator with the box resting at my feet, sweat soaking my shirt's thin weave.

"Yeah, but if I tell her about it, then she'll convince me to stay," says my mother.

"Do you want to stay?"

The door opens. I step inside, sliding the box with my foot. I hit the tenth-floor button, but the button doesn't light up, so I wave my key card in front of the sensor and mash it again.

"I told you, I love her," my mom says.

"It sounds like you hate her."

The elevator stops on the third floor.

"She wants me to live with her. She wants to take care of me. She basically asks me to work fewer hours so that she can take me on lavish vacations, then she transfers money into my bank account to keep me dependent on her. I tell her not to, but she does it anyway."

"Sounds kind of nice."

The doors open, and a security guard steps inside, holding an empty sandwich bag. He smiles at me and checks the buttons. He mashes the door-close button and the doors close.

"I'll be in St. Petersburg next weekend getting boxes from your nana's storage unit. I had to talk to your father."

"Did he say anything about Butters?" It's been over a month, and I suddenly realize I haven't checked on her.

The elevator stops at the sixth floor and the doors open. No one is there. The security guard presses the door-close button and the doors close again.

"What do you mean?" says my mother.

"She was sick when I left."

"Yeah."

"What did the vet say?"

We reach the tenth floor and the doors open. Standing before us are the thriller writer, another security guard, and a middle-aged woman in tweed, displaying my panties on the eraser end of a pencil.

"Baby, Butters is dead."

THERE'S AN INVESTIGATION into who trespassed into Karen's cubicle. She relinquishes her last piece of evidence, my panties, to the security guard's bag as I eavesdrop from the kitchen. I overhear him say he'll review the closed-circuit footage from the previous night. "I'll be honest, ma'am. It was probably a sex worker."

Before he leaves, he circulates the floor and asks the rest of us to report any suspicious activity, anyone we've noticed who doesn't seem to belong.

I stay for an hour after everyone leaves. My plan was to write, but instead I apply for ten jobs I won't get. I find most of them on the NYFA website. I debate making another Keurig, but I decide it would be better to go home instead and spend time with Seth. He's been upset since his hours at Dick Blick were cut in half a week ago, for unstated reasons. I figure it's either his petty shoplifting of art supplies or his difficult personality. It's obvious when he dislikes someone, and he sulks when he doesn't feel like doing something.

I put my laptop in its slipcase and zip my backpack. I take my phone out of the front pocket and see that Brian has texted me. It's been weeks since our last conversation. **Did you tell anyone about us?** the message says.

I stare at it. I've continued writing him letters but stopped mailing them. The silence of the office spreads around me, and the light above my desk shines directly down on my head. I feel Seth's location almost an hour away like a rope pulled taut. There's no question of not answering. I should do so now, while I'm still alone.

No, I say. **Why?**

I hold my phone in my lap and stare into the weave of my cubicle wall.

Erin says everyone knows, he says. **Claudette told her.**

Claudette wouldn't, I say, but I don't know that. My friendship with Claudette, while close, is an outgrowth of my relationship with Seth via Jared. Should there be a conflict of interest, I have no doubt Seth will take precedence over me. Along with Seth will go all of my friends, my plans for the future, my residence, the money I've invested in our new living arrangement. **What did you say to Erin?**

Nothing. That she was lying, he says.

I take out my laptop and open it on the desk. I message Erin on Facebook to ask if she's spoken about me with Claudette recently, and include my phone number. I close my laptop. My hands shake as I call Claudette.

"I don't know what you're talking about," she says.

"There's nothing to know."

"Okay."

"Erin is just jealous because Brian called me for comfort when he found out she was fucking his best friend."

"Why did he call you, of all people?"

"Erin's calling me," I say. "I'll call you back."

"Well, aren't you?" says Erin.

"No," I say. I leave my body as I speak. I don't know what I say. I force my tone to remain calm. I try to use big words because I doubt she'll understand them. "I would appreciate it if you didn't perpetuate this rumor," I say.

"I saw the video, Nina."

"What video?"

She laughs. I wait. "You don't know about this?" she says.

"I have no idea what you're talking about." I run my hands over the surface of my memory. They come back clean.

"There are dozens of them, not just you," she says. "There's one of a girl who looks like she could be fifteen. I found them on his computer and then on a kink website in his browser history."

I stare at my reflection in the floor-to-ceiling window behind my cube. The lights of the office across the street obscure my eyes. "Whatever you saw wasn't me."

"It was definitely you."

"What website?"

"It doesn't matter. The internet is forever."

"It wasn't me," I say. "You're wrong, and I don't want you talking to anyone else about this."

"At least you're not the only one," she says. "Don't worry, I won't tell your boyfriend."

SETH HAS BORROWED my copy of *Journey to the Center of the Earth*. He's been reading it for the last three days that he hasn't been working, and he's reading it now on our bed, in his underwear, the same pair he wore yesterday. So far, he's made no mention of looking for a way to supplement his halved income. It doesn't seem to concern him that he won't make his part of the rent this month. Nor has he told Rafael. "It doesn't concern him," he says.

"Hey," I say, casually exhausted. I drop my bag in the doorway. He doesn't look up. "How was your day?"

He nods. His indifference tells me he doesn't know what happened. On the subway, I deleted every message I have ever exchanged with Brian: Facebook, Gchat, Twitter, Instagram. My eyes travel nonchalantly over to the wooden box of notebooks where I've hidden the bundle of unsent letters. It appears undisturbed.

"I have to go to the bathroom and then there's something I need to talk to you about."

"Do you," he says.

I float to the bathroom. I sit on the closed lid of the toilet and press my hands together over my mouth. I breathe in the warm air of my own breath and press my knuckles into my eyelids and feel totally out of control. I stare into the grout. I notice a half-smoked bowl on the edge of the bathtub, hit it three times, and let the numb settle in. The white noise mutes, and I lift the toilet lid and empty my intestines into the bowl. They're liquid.

Back in the bedroom, I feel lighter. I assume my position on the bed. Seth isn't even halfway through the novel, and it crosses my mind that he may have an undiagnosed learning disability. Or perhaps he's on the spectrum. Or maybe it's simply a function of being a two-dimensional artist: that, as in a painting, his thoughts move laterally across a plane rather than progressing linearly, one after the other. In the yellow light, I'm able to find it endearing, fascinating even.

I say calmly, "There's a rumor that Brian and I are sleeping together. Whatever you hear, it isn't true. Erin made it up because she's jealous. Brian and I are friends."

I await his reaction. He looks at a spot just above my eyes.

"I told you the other day, Brian and Erin have been talking again lately. It turns out she's been sleeping with Jasper. This is their drama, not mine."

He closes the book and sets it gently between us. "Please don't take this the wrong way, Nina."

I show him I'm listening.

"I know you read into things. Historically, you tend to make impulsive decisions based upon your immediate desires."

Don't speak, I think. *Don't say anything.*

"You don't consider the consequences."

"What are you talking about?" I say.

"Listen. I know I've pushed you away. I've held you responsible for my own fear-based projections. However—"

"Are you about to say that you believe this disgusting rumor?"

"If the rumor is true, it's my own fault for enabling you, for failing to take control of my life."

"Enabling me in what way? What are you talking about? You're contradicting yourself."

"Please don't get defensive."

"I'm not getting defensive, Seth. I'm genuinely confused."

"You're a conveniently confused girl. You have male baggage and a unique perspective on the world that only favors yourself."

"I mean, everyone is the center of their own universe," I say, pretending to laugh. "What do you mean, 'male baggage'?"

"I know you."

"Debatable." My mind is white. "Brian and I are friends."

"Oh, I'm sure you're great friends. And if the rumor is true, I'm pretty powerless to do anything about it."

"I can't believe you're saying this."

"You decide you want something, and it might as well be chiseled in marble."

"I didn't do anything."

"You don't like to be criticized. You don't like to be told you're wrong."

"Stop telling me who I am."

"You would be happier without someone around to show you the consequences of your actions. You can't stand to feel guilty about your consistently selfish choices."

"Stop telling me who I am."

"I wish you had a better understanding of what a relationship means for me. You know I lost my father and my mother quickly moved on. I have had a complicated life."

"I do understand what a relationship means for you. I haven't done anything to compromise that."

"Even if you had, you would feel no obligation to tell me about it. It's not in your nature. You think only of yourself."

I grab a pair of scissors from the jar on the nightstand. They're brand-new and extremely sharp. I dig an open point into the flesh of my wrist and drag it toward my elbow, looking Seth in the eye. It makes a white ditch that quickly fills with blood.

"Stop. Telling me. Who. I am," I say.

THE GASH THROBS. It throbs as I see a man beating his meat on the sidewalk. It throbs as I walk several blocks away from the thriller writer's office to pick up his lunch. I wear long sleeves to conceal the wound even though it's 98 degrees outside and my shirt presses hot exhaust into my skin. Everyone on line at the Chop't on Lexington is wearing black. I hand the thriller writer his roughage, and it throbs as he compares the receipt against his change. He asks me for loyalty when I say that I'm quitting, but I tell him I need more money. "I thought your parents were helping you," he says. It throbs as I turn away.

It throbs as I ask Seth to change my bandage. We sit on the edge of the bathtub, and I play the part of his patient, weeping as he ties his hair into a bun. He bows over the flesh, unbinding the gauze, and pauses when the thread catches on scab. "Sorry," he says.

"It doesn't hurt."

He dabs it with ointment. He covers it and binds it with medical tape, sits very still when he's finished, and looks me in the eye. I'm enjoying the prolonged revenge for what he's done to me. I can tell that he's scared of me. I wallow in the unnameable longing I feel in the throb. Self-destruction is my trump card. I blame him for it. In my heart, I know I'm a caring person, with a desire not to harm.

eleven

By fall, I've fully entered the gig economy. I'm an art model, a free-lance editor, a dog walker, a part-time assistant, a babysitter, and a movie extra. I find these jobs through friends of friends, on Craigslist, on Facebook, on flyers posted at public libraries and around Bed-Stuy. I wake at six each morning to find more of them. I feel as if I'm always gasping, always moving, never sleeping. I begin to feel a deep sense of hatred for the hustle; I see the hustle as a form of violence wielded against me by late-stage capitalism. I see it in the drawn face of every body surrounding me on the G train at seven in the morning. I have no free time and no job security, so when a West Village bookstore calls me for an interview, I'm gleeful.

The bookstore basement is papered in faux leather-bounds. The receiving desk is piled high with galleys. The owner sees me eyeing one by Jonathan Franzen and tries to give it to me. "Oh, no thank you," I say.

The owner is a few years older than I am, tall and ethereal like Gwyneth Paltrow. Her name is also Nina, but she's obviously a superior breed of Nina. She holds a copy of my résumé and asks me whom I'm studying with in my MFA program. I name my professors.

"Hm, I don't know them," she says, cocking her head.

She asks me what I like to read. I name a few contemporary authors I saw on *Electric Literature* this morning, and then one rather obscure name from the past. "I also read everything published by New Directions," I say. In truth, I'm reading *The Seven Principles for Making Marriage Work*. On the cover, the *O* of "*Work*" is comprised of two shiny gold rings in a Venn diagram. I've encouraged Seth to read it, too, but thus far he's shown no interest. I'm sure he feels the self-help genre is beneath him, or perhaps that I'm the problem with our relationship, not he. His mother has paid his last two months' rent since Blick cut him out of the schedule entirely without technically firing him so he can't collect unemployment. Seth's mother has told him she won't pay for another month. He thinks she's bluffing. "What looks like idleness to her is integral to the creative process," he tells me. He says he's taking steps toward building himself a website. When he shows it to me, there is no contact information on it. "If they want to find me, they'll know how," he says.

"Are you available to start next week?" asks Nina, and I almost kiss her. She makes me a manager with three closing shifts, a lanyard, and a set of keys. She offers me fourteen dollars an hour with insurance, but I already have insurance through my school. "You can sign up when you graduate," she says.

Though the thriller writer's new book hit the bestseller list, I quickly learn that no one at the bookstore has ever heard of him, so I stop saying his name. I start saying the names of books that are coming out this week when I'm asked what I'm reading. I reorder the same titles each Sunday, based on my sections' sales; if a book hasn't sold in four weeks, I don't restock it. I shelve the books that accumulate behind the registers, new shipments waiting to be shelved or customers' leave-behinds. I start having dreams about running operations in the store's DOS inventory system.

I rail against Amazon on the store's Twitter and make signage for the rotating table displays with themes like the true history of

Thanksgiving, philosophers and the poets they inspired, and new works in translation.

I let the other booksellers trade shifts with me to attend marches and die-ins and let anarchist book clubs host meetings in the Sociology & Politics section, where I shelve and listen in on their discussions of Hannah Arendt, and dialectics.

I straighten the sideline items and direct people to the bathroom. I advise them what to buy for their frenemy's birthday or their kid's preschool graduation or their honeymoon in Laos. I count the tills when we close. Behind the registers and bookshelves, on the shared computers in the basement, on bathroom and cigarette and free-coffee breaks, any spare moment that I can find, all day, I am talking to Aaron.

AARON AND I have continued sleeping together whenever we're alone. This happens more frequently now as he's currently production-assisting for a movie directed by Greta Gerwig, shooting near the bookstore. I steal postcards from the impulse rack, doodle on them, then mail them to Aaron's parents' house on Staten Island. I point him out to my coworkers, joking, "If I weren't with Seth, I'd fuck him." He browses the Used shelf and waits for my shifts to finish. He's outside the store when I'm locking up. Christmas season has brought the first snow, coating the cobblestones, and Aaron hands me a plastic shopping bag. It's from the bookstore. "I got this for you," he says.

The book is wrapped in brown butcher paper, tied with a black ribbon. It's a worn green hardcover with *The Hollow Earth* printed in gold on its spine. The author's name has rubbed off, so I flip to the title page: *Dr. Raymond Bernard, A.B., M.A., Ph.D. for Bell*

Publishing Company of New York. 1979. The Greatest Geological Discovery in History. Made by Admiral Richard E. Byrd in the Mysterious Land Beyond the Poles. The True Origin of the Flying Saucers.

"There's an official history, and then there's the true story," he says. "The seen and the unseen."

"This is amazing."

I flip through the pages. They're cream and brittle. I hadn't known it would snow, and I'm shivering in ballet flats and a light jacket with no gloves. We move beneath the awning, and I read by the window light. I'm aware of how the setting lends our rendezvous a cinematic quality. *February, 1947: "I'd like to see that land beyond the Pole. That area beyond the Pole is the center of the Great Unknown."*

"Can I drive you home?" he says.

HE HOLDS MY hand in the car as we cross the Brooklyn Bridge and weave silently through empty streets to Bed-Stuy. At the top of my block, we find the street cordoned off with yellow police tape and matching evidence tags mapping out a path to a smashed-up police cruiser on the opposite side of the street, its window shattered across the asphalt. An officer waves us through to the next block, and we creep around, craning our necks in the rearview mirrors to see a cluster of other uniforms bending over the mess, going all the way up to the subway entrance. Neighbors are leaning out of their windows above store awnings. "I wonder what happened," I say as I lower my head to take Aaron in my mouth. I feel the windows looking down on me as he keeps his hand on my hair. He cums in my throat, and I kiss him and continue swallowing the rest of the way to my door. He follows me in his car. Police lights cycle faintly on the face of my building. Our bedroom window is dark, so Seth is asleep.

I stop on the landing to remember Aaron's hands, his mouth, his hair, his spit, the yeast of his crotch. I rub my lip and my thoughts quickly turn to panic. I slip to the bathroom and sit on the edge of the tub, rummaging through my backpack as the room fills with steam. I strip off my clothes. My toes burn lowering into the water. *Why have the Poles never been reached?* I read, smoking. *No Poles exist in the sense usually understood.*

I place the book facedown on the bath mat. The water drains, and I stare at a fresh Lady Bic on the windowsill. *Why does the sun not appear for so long a time in winter near the supposed Poles?* I break it open to remove the razor and guide it into my hip. I wipe the blood on my fingertip and taste it. I stand in a towel, gazing into the condensation of the mirror.

As one passes over the rim of the polar opening and approaches the earth's interior, one sinks inward into the hollow. I slide the book under our bed, then fish my phone out of my bag and text Aaron, I **appreciate you**. I lie down beside Seth. His hair is wet and smells of tea tree. I can tell by the tension in his body that he's awake but doesn't want to talk to me. "I love you," I say. He doesn't answer.

The next morning, I Google the news in Bed-Stuy and learn that two on-duty police officers were shot at point-blank range on the next block. The shooter was seeking revenge for Eric Garner and Michael Brown. He hadn't targeted them specifically. Any two officers would do.

"I kind of see his reasoning," I say to Seth as he makes us eggs-in-a-basket. "It's random and unfair."

"And he's clearly crazy," he says.

"Is he?"

"Isn't he?"

"But do you see what I'm saying? It's bound to happen."

He ran into the subway and killed himself. He would have died anyway—they would have shot him if he hadn't.

THERE'S ICE ON the ground when Brian comes to visit his mother in Bay Ridge. I agree to meet him at a coffee shop on the corner where the cops were shot. I suggest the location expecting him not to agree to it since it's over an hour away, but he does. A few months have passed since my conversation with Erin, and I haven't asked Brian about the video. We don't talk anymore. It's been easier to pretend that I don't know what I know, to place that night in a black hole in my memory. Brian's seeming contentedness on Instagram, his clubbing, his hiking, his soccer tournaments, allow me to believe that Erin's story may have come from a place of malice. I have no way to confirm. I'm distantly relieved to see that he's extricated himself from that toxic situation. I tell myself that I'm happy we're able to catch up like old friends. He stands from the table and hugs me when I arrive. He tells me about his forays on Tinder. We laugh. I tell him Seth and I have been happier lately, since I sent him some *Psychology Today* articles on nonviolent communication.

"I had a feeling it was rough between you," he says. "Why didn't you talk to me about it?"

"I didn't want to burden you," I say.

"You wouldn't have." He smiles sadly. "You helped me so much through my breakup with Erin. We don't talk anymore, by the way."

"I figured."

"She and Jasper got handfasted."

I already know. Claudette went to the ceremony. She posted the pictures on Facebook. Erin looked pregnant, but I decide against aiming the conversation in this direction. "How's your mom?" I say.

"Good," he says. "She's good."

"Have you thought any more about the test?"

"The test?"

"The test," I say, but there's no recognition. I look at my phone and make like I have to leave suddenly. "I'm sorry," I say.

"Don't go," he says. He touches my knee. "I'm sorry. I just don't want to talk about that."

"Okay."

"I wasn't going to tell you, but I decided to get the test after our conversation," he says. "Then, when we stopped talking, I realized I couldn't. The doctors wouldn't let me anymore because I didn't have someone to stay with me. I need someone to do this with me. I knew you would see me today because you care about me, Nina. I know you do. I know you'll always be there for me. Do you mind if we go back to your apartment and talk in private?"

"I don't think we should do that."

"It's not like that," he says. "I just need to take a shower. Please. I'm so filthy from the subway. I swear I just want to shower."

I TELL BRIAN he has half an hour. He comes into our apartment and walks coolly to the shower. I sit on a wooden barstool next to the plywood table and am moved by the obviousness of his display. I stare at the white of the back of the bathroom door. Hear the sigh of the shower opening. Seth is out with Paolo, and I fantasize about him barging in at this very moment, what he would think of my explanation that Brian is only here to bathe himself. Whether this scene, of my declining to join him in that activity, would exonerate me of my sins.

We walk to the subway together afterward, and Brian's clean hand reaches for mine. I let him take it. I tell myself that this is what friends do: friends hold hands. He stands with me at the turnstile, vulnerable, disbelieving. I realize he is lonely. His loneliness soothes me. We hug and there is hesitation in his embrace. I press into him. "I'm sure we'll see each other again soon," I say.

"Yeah," he says. "It's not that, though."

I search his face. I have a sudden urge to flee and an opposing urge to cling. The train is coming and I glance at the tracks, signaling to him that I have to go. He leans in to kiss me on the corner of my mouth, and I let him, and the train is screaming as I swipe myself through. I check my phone when I sit. He's already texted me.

Thank you.

For what?

For being my support. You're right. It's better to know.

THE MEMORY OF Brian's skin smelling of soap lives everywhere in my body as I close the bookstore. His dark, wet hair and the bathroom steam spilling into the common area. Brian naked on the wooden stool before me, asking me with his eyes to touch him. My resistance. His flight takes off in three hours, and it's an hour to JFK. I have sixty dollars in my bank account, and there's a *Rolling Stone* photography book I decide I need to give him for Christmas. I text Seth to say that I'm going out with a coworker. I text Brian to say I'll be at the airport. You're the last woman I made love to, he responds. I want you to be the next.

The train is empty all the way to the airport. Brian's Uber is stuck in traffic. I wait near the bathrooms at the Delta check-in, bathed in fluorescence and sanitized bacteria. He arrives and proceeds directly to the kiosk. I come up behind him. "There's a problem with my reservation," he says, and he tells me to get in line. The line is out the door. He isn't sure what to do with me now that I'm here; he won't look at me. I hand him the bag with the book in it. I touch his waist.

"You want me to open this now?" he says.

"I'm just giving it to you."

He sets it on the ground by his suitcase.

"You're welcome," I say. We kiss. "I love you, you know."

I'm pulled by the inertia of the weight of my confession: I know it's true because I hadn't planned to say it. My heart begins racing and I repeat it with more conviction.

His eyes are dark and nervous. "I know you do."

I TELL SETH I don't know myself sexually. I say I need to explore. He's framed by the camouflage net curtains he's hung over the two windows, on either side of our bed. He stares at a place above my eyes, and it's as if a movie is being projected onto my forehead in which I am sucking Brian's dick in the men's disabled stall at the Delta terminal. I'm on my knees where strange men shit, toilets flushing around me, and until that moment, I've been in a fugue state, thinking I'm in love with him. I awake from it in medias res, aware I am being used. I have the distinct sense of starring in shame porn. "Choke on it," Brian is saying. "Take it all the way into your throat."

Seth ashes his cigarette out the window. It blows back inside. "Be honest with me," he says. "Is it that I have a lower sex drive than you?"

"No," I say. I try to sound certain. I lick the sticky film of Brian's cum, lingering in my mouth. "I just want to try different things with you."

"I know Jared holds certain beliefs about love and fidelity," he says. "I don't subscribe to them."

"I don't want to be polyamorous," I say.

"Then what is it?"

"I guess I want you to be more aggressive."

He finishes the cigarette. I watch him, considering the possibility that this is not a problem with the relationship, that therefore I cannot fix it from within. I immerse myself in the fear of losing him. Of him hating me. Of living on the streets, friendless and dirty. He drags the cigarette back and forth across the windowsill. He throws the butt outside.

"You're a very sexual person, Nina. I sometimes wonder what you would be able to do with your energy if you weren't so focused on your sexual preoccupations."

"I just think there should be variety in what we do together. This can only help us in the long term," I say.

"What kind of variety? Specifically what do you want me to do?"

"You could tie me up, maybe."

He stares into the bookshelf.

"Would you want to do that?" I say.

"Is that what you want me to do?" he says. He rises from the bed.

"What do you want?"

"What I want, Nina . . ." He paces. "What I want doesn't matter, because you'll find a way to satisfy yourself with or without me."

"Take that back," I say.

"You're not a bad person. This is just who you are."

"Who am I?" I say, growing agitated. I pray that he says something generous.

"I think you're afraid to answer that truthfully."

I hurl a book at the window. I want it to shatter, but it doesn't; the book thuds stupidly. I walk to the closet, step inside it, and slam the door. I remember that Rafael is at a show tonight and open the door and slam it two more times.

"Nina, what are you doing?"

I tell him to kill himself. Something breaks, and I know it's Paolo's vase, and I feel elated. I sit in the laundry basket, keeping my hands on the knob. Seth's footsteps grow closer. I hear him gathering the pieces. He puts his hand on the other side. I fight him against it. I tell him he's crazy. "I'll tell everyone you hit me," I say.

"Come out," he says.

"Get away from me," I say. I open the door and punch myself in the face. "Am I selfish?" I say. "Am I?"

"Stop it." He reaches for my fist.

"Don't fucking touch me."

I punch him in the chest. He gives up and I climb back into the closet and sit in the laundry basket, weeping.

"You build the world with your words, Nina," he says.

There's a soft click of the door.

twelve

I call Seth from the bookstore and tell him, honestly, that I'll be
staying with a coworker through the rainy season. I can't break up
with him to his face; I am tired of looking at him. I keep our conversation brief despite his pleading. I act as if I'm surprised that he's
surprised. My gut tells me he's mostly worried about where he'll live
now, so I offer to pay my third of the rent until our lease is up in
August. That I'm gracious enough to do this instead of rendering
him homeless underscores how petty it is that every day afterward
he threatens via text to "put my effects on the curb."

I've brought nothing with me from Bed-Stuy. Leonard's extra
room is a closet with a window and a daybed; there's no room for
my things. I have my box of journals and clothes enough to fill a
set of plastic rolling drawers. I remind Seth that I sent him Listings
Project emails, Craigslist postings, names of friends of friends to aid
in his job hunt. He'd said he'd follow up on them, then let the conversations die, or forgot to respond, or declined to make plans. People
were unimpressed with him, and therefore unimpressed with me; it
was humiliating.

The problem as Seth wanted me to understand it was that he is
an artistic genius and has a fundamentally harder time feeling mo-
tivated to do anything but make his art. So I asked my father if his
creative agency would hire him.

"He's taking on more freelance work," I said. It was the first time I'd talked to my father since I found out he put Butters to sleep without telling me. "I didn't want to upset you," he explained at the time, so I took some space from him to think about that. The space had lasted weeks.

"What's his experience?"

I'd counseled Seth that he might need to learn new skills. "What kind of work do you have?" I asked. "He can do a lot of things."

He told me to have him send his portfolio. Seth commenced curating one, drawing from his various projects to give my father a sense of his range. He included favorite pieces from his "archive" at the coffee shop. Some sketches from his journal. His solo show at Black Box, as the artist-in-residence. Some cell phone photos of his Woven series, still in progress. When the time came to send his portfolio, he told me he was uncomfortable doing it on his own behalf. So I sent it for him. Then I followed up.

"Does he have any experience with Adobe Suite?" said my father.

"He prefers more traditional modes."

"I can't help him."

"What if he were a consultant?"

"What would I need to consult with him about?"

I put the phone down and examined my fingers. With my left two incisors, I tore off the cuticle of my thumb. I chewed it and swallowed. My father thought Seth was a fool. I came back to the phone. "How does he learn Adobe Suite?" I said.

"Have you ever heard the saying 'Time kills deals'? Seth doesn't want to work. If he did, he'd be doing it."

My father didn't pursue my mother when she left. I thought she would have wanted him to, and this made me furious with him. I threw temper tantrums, hurling myself against the walls of my bedroom. I overturned furniture. I woke in night sweats and wet the bed for two years in high school. I demanded my father's attention; I knew that if I failed to pursue him, he would lose interest in me.

"He's decided it's not worth making a change, because making a change involves effort and thought," said my father. "He'd rather do things the way he's always done them. What you did is you let Seth get off the hook."

"This is victim-blaming."

"Time kills deals, Nina. People can always find reasons not to close."

I was a straight-A student in the Den of Inquiry. Even as I signed myself into rehab with my father beside me, handing over his insurance card, my performance of it was practical: I wanted him to see that my addiction was a problem I would swiftly ameliorate and put behind me. I have always been aware that I am the only chance my father has to be a father. If I fuck up my life again, then my father has fucked up. Like him, and for him, when need be, I must be cold and solution-oriented.

PLEASE TELL ME why this is hard for you, Seth says. We've texted every day since I left. When we talk on the phone, I scream at him. Seth doesn't think I'm grieving him, and I'm not, but I want him to think that I am. I feel nothing for him now, a week after leaving him. I can't imagine letting him touch me—I feel repelled by the memory of his dick. I'm embarrassed that I was ever impressed by it, but I had such low expectations then. I feel callous and I don't want to feel callous. I miss you, I say. But I've never been alone. There's always been someone in my life taking me away from myself. I hope you understand.

I understand that you want to be with Aaron, he says.

I breathe from my diaphragm. I imagine myself floating above this nonsense. Seth doesn't know that I'm spending time with Aaron. I've seen Aaron every day since leaving him, but Seth is guessing at that; he has no way to confirm it. When he asks me what I do with my time now, I enjoy reminding him that it's none of his business, that he's no longer entitled to that information. I don't ask him what he's doing, do I? I don't care.

I respond, I'm trying to be open with you.

I feel sad for you, Nina, he says. And your demented, twisted, destructive idea of a relationship.

Sorry you feel that way.

I wish I'd never met you. I've spent weeks unraveling all the bizarre lines of bullshit you fed me. Your warped morals and justifications. I wish you the best. You're a queer girl.

You too.

With enough work and enough support, you can learn to stop hurting others, much as you've learned to stop hurting yourself.

Goodbye, Seth.

Do you know I shouldn't even be talking to you, Nina? You're beneath me and you're not. We're both abnormal. That's what attracted us to each other.

Interesting theory.

Yes, sorry you think this means we can't be together. I also see the reasons, but I was holding out hope that people can change. You're a shining example that they don't.

I mute him without responding. I decide yet again that I don't care. When I left Seth alone in that nasty apartment that he wasn't paying for, I felt a new version of myself taking over. She was ruthless and immune to his mind games. The last vestiges of love lifted like a veil as I rode the D train to Leonard's house that first night, cleansed myself in his standing shower, and leaned against his island counter to tell him my version of the story. I felt horribly free. I was able to grow in any direction I wanted to. I could be whoever I wanted to be. I imagined living alone in the woods, a hermit writing outsider novels.

I called Claudette the following morning and said very simply, "Seth and I broke up." I tried to sound mature, like I hadn't acted out of impulse or done anything to harm him, per se—like I respected and cared for him, and thought separating was in his best interest, too. It should speak to my character that I didn't disparage him. "It hasn't been working for a long time," I said. "I just want to end the conflict. I want us to be friends. When we're ready."

She was quiet. I watched Leonard come out of the shower and walk across the apartment in his towel. "Are you even upset about it?" she said.

I was operating at a certain remove from my own emotions. I may have sounded cruel, but I simply wanted her to understand that in no way did I blame Seth for our disunion, publicly. "Of course. I'm not a sociopath."

I WISH TO acknowledge my indebtedness to the brave men who have spent their time, comfort and, in many cases, have given their lives, so that all may know the truth and geography of this wonderful planet. For days after leaving, I bring books from the bookstore home to Leonard's and stack them against the walls. With access to silence, I aspire to read titles by Clarice Lispector, Thomas Bernhard, and Frantz Fanon on the recommendations of more talented students in my MFA program, but I never open these books. Instead

I keep *The Hollow Earth* by my bedside. *I claim that the earth is not only hollow, but that all explorers who spent time past the rim of the polar opening have had a look into the interior.* I've abandoned my novel. I imagined having my own space would lubricate productivity, but when I sit down alone with myself now, I hear nothing; it's as if I've lost the walls against which ideas resonate. I write the same lines over and over. In my closet of a bedroom, I spend hours staring into the void of my computer, desperate for something to fill it. I text Aaron and tell him to come over, and he arrives in the early morning after leaving the set. I say we need to work on our script, so we sit on the daybed and write dialogue together. "'I'm writing a book, Tina,'" I say.

"'What's your book called?'" he says.

"'I'm calling it *I Want It All*. It's a working title.'"

"'Sounds like a long book.'"

"'It is. It's about everything I want.'" We laugh. He types for a while and I watch him, comforted that his collaboration will shepherd me back to myself. I feel no need to perform for him.

"I can see what you'll look like when you're old," I tell him.

"I was born old," he says.

I imagine us being the only two people in this wretched asshole of a world. We're so very alone here, lonelier all the time. Jared's last email to me read: *Having been placed non-consensually betwixt y'all in a delicate situation, I've witnessed both parties commit a series of self-focused, not to say selfish, acts of poor listening and, thus it follows, poor communication.* He sent it the morning after I sucked Brian's dick in the disabled stall. I read it behind the register at the bookstore, and felt my friends and my self-respect peeling away like dead skin. *I need to know honestly,* he said, *I request facts because Seth distorts them, unintentionally, and I can't do what he needs*

*me to do, namely help him calm down and think, if I don't know truth
from fiction—do you want to sleep with other people?*

I had always known there was no neutrality. I saw this message
beginning the domino effect of collapsing everything I love. Every social outcome has been in Seth's favor. I no longer hear from
Claudette. I haven't communicated with Theo since telling him that
Numina was no longer something my schedule could accommodate;
that I could not, for no money, find him a new unpaid editor. Who
knows what rumors circulate about me thirdhand through the bars
of St. Petersburg. I am Lilith. I am Jezebel.

Thank you for this unsolicited feedback, I responded.

"Nina, I'm sick of taking out trash on other people's sets," says
Aaron, checking his phone. It's four in the morning and he has to be
on set at eight. It's over an hour to Staten Island.

"That's why we're writing this script," I say. "Stay over. Don't go
back tonight."

"Are you sure?"

"Of course."

"What about Leonard?"

My room has two doors: one leads to the hallway; the other leads
to Leonard's room. I sometimes hear him turning over in bed.

"I don't think he would mind," I say.

Leonard is the bookstore's security guard and has wanted to sleep
with me since he found me crying on my cigarette break. I pay him
each morning for the kindness he's shown me by eating oatmeal in
my boxers and sports bra on his recliner. I experience a brief sus-
pension of reality as I make love to Aaron on Leonard's daybed and
imagine him listening, jerking off, cumming on his fist. It is quiet
but for springs and breathing. I have the sense that he smells us when
Aaron goes down on me and I soak the mattress in warm urea. We

leave the window open for ventilation. Aaron is gone before dawn, and I drift through the following workday, the following night, and every night after, as he comes, and comes over, and comes, and comes again, over and over and over.

WE CARRY MY boxes down four flights of stairs from the Bed-Stuy apartment and load them into Aaron's car. *I'm sorry to hear you had problems with the neighborhood,* my landlord said when I emailed her about returning the deposit. "Nikki is going to wire the money to me," I tell Rafael, the last of us there, with his single blue bin of belongings. He nods but doesn't look at me. Seth has talked to him, I'm sure has bled his heart out for Rafael on my account. "Hey, do you have, like, ten dollars of weed I can buy from you?" I say.

"Just take this," he says, handing me a plastic baggie from his pocket.

"I couldn't," I say, but I do. It's rude not to. I never cared about Rafael's friendship, anyway. I've always considered him, as a white spoken-word poet, a little bit racist. I never went to the Nuyorican with him, despite his invitations, plural. That space is not mine. "Thanks, man."

We drive my boxes to Aaron's parents' house on Staten Island. He's told me they can stay in the garage until I find a place or we find a place. It seems inevitable that we'll end up living together, as if it's not entirely within our control, as if it's the only fiscally responsible choice and the only self-respecting choice Aaron has. Over the course of nearly a month, we've become a unit. We make plans jointly, make plans for the not-too-distant future, are easy collaborators.

His parents' house is two stories with a soft green yard, and hydrangeas with rabbits underneath. There's a literal white picket fence separating their house from the neighbors', but it stops before the street. His mother is at the stove making spaghetti Bolognese when we come inside. She's a peach-colored woman, shorter and wider than I. She greets me skeptically as if she knows something about me just by looking at me, or knows nothing about me at all, and had no idea I was coming, but considers it mildly inconvenient yet typical.

I have the immediate sense that the family is secular, faithless, though Aaron has told me that for a period he went to Catholic school. Coming from the South, I'm accustomed to seeing at least one crucifix over the kitchen sink, even in the homes of families who never attend church—even my mother has one, and even her special friend identifies as a born-again Christian, and listens to the Christian radio station, and goes to Christian rock concerts: it's an aesthetic more than a true belief system. But the walls of Aaron's parents' house are decorated with Italian ceramics and photos of Aaron and his brother as small children. There's a hideous yellow credenza displaying gaudy Venetian clowns in the sitting room.

Aaron's mother pauses suddenly in her stirring and places her hand over her stomach. "Are you okay?" Aaron says, peering down into her face, grasping both of her shoulders. I feel a pang of jealousy watching them. There's something incestuous about it.

"Just my stomach," she says.

"Are you unwell?" he says. "Can I get you a Tums?"

He hurries away before she can answer. We're left alone in the kitchen, and I feel pressured to say something about Aaron to his mother, since he is all we have in common. She looks at me.

"Aaron says you're a teacher," I say, using my good-girl voice.

She nods and says, "And what do you do?"

"I work in a bookstore," I say weakly. Aaron returns. He displays four Tums in the palm of his hand. I have the urge to validate myself to his mother already and feel strangely infantilized by my relation to her as her child's peer. There is bad energy in her attitude toward me. She probably thinks I'm the kind of person who moves back in with her parents and thus does not deserve her son, all the while judging me poorly for dating a person who has moved back in with his parents. Will I betray her sweet precious baby when I learn how pathetic he is? I dread her discovering that I've been to rehab. I can tell she's the kind of person who's never seen a therapist.

"Set the table, will you?" she says to Aaron. "You got a speeding ticket." She says this as if the two ideas are related. She gestures toward the Formica counter at a pile of junk mail. She has a faint Queens accent and a way of becoming the thing around which every body in a room orbits. "You understand what you do in that car goes on your father's driving record, not yours."

"Yes, I know that," he says.

"But we're not paying your speeding tickets."

"Yes, I know that, Mother."

"DO YOU HAVE a way to pay these people?" says Aaron's father. We've just finished telling them about our plans to shoot the movie. We've reached the dessert portion of the meal, where Aaron has set out an array of cookies and decaf, and seltzer he made a show of preparing in the SodaStream. I see Aaron's dynamic in the family as very childlike, and it gives me unrest considering it's understood that we are moving in together, but I also know that I need him. A partner is a conduit for conducting a certain dimension of one's experience, a way to collage and create oneself, like a walking, breathing search engine: it's expedient to have one, affords one's life content and depth and authority and direction. Plus I have no idea how to do it alone. What steps do I take, with my income, my inexperience? How do I find a roommate? What if I don't like that person? What if they're a serial killer? What if I run out of money? What if I'm forced to move out and I don't have a windfall? What if I step into the empty street and trip and fall, and am laughed at? What if I'm hit by a Mack truck and no one can identify me? What if there is no one around to see me not doing the dishes, farting in my underwear, or saying I don't have time for them and locking myself in the bathroom, or waking up grouchy at them for no reason? Will I disappear? How will I know which movies to watch, which books to read, which albums are coming out, which shows are opening? What if Aaron is mad at me for saying no?

"How are you going to pay for this without a producer?" says his mother. "Not out of pocket, I know that. You're not putting it on a credit card, because you know who'd end up paying for it."

"I didn't ask you to pay for anything."

"You never have in the past, either."

"What do your parents do?" his father asks me.

"My father is an entrepreneur," I say. "My mother is a bartender."

"An entrepreneur," says his mother, smiling at his father.

"What do you do?" I say.

"I generate ad content for political campaigns," he says.

"That's something else you need to think about," says his mother. "Advertising for your movie. Who's going to pay for that?"

"Can you stop?" says Aaron.

"What? What did I say?" She looks at me.

"I hate to say it, but she's right," says his father.

"Can you guys stop?"

"You should be using this time to look for a job," says his mother.

"I know it's hard for you to understand this, but this is me looking for a job."

"Really? It's going to pay your rent when you finally move out?"

"It's looking for a job in the long term."

"Oh, because it seems to me like you're thinking very short-term."

Aaron stands from the table and leaves abruptly. We watch the empty door frame as he stomps down the hallway and up the stairs, and slams his bedroom door several times. His mother looks at his father with a self-satisfied smile, shaking her head in disbelief. "How do you like that?" she says to me.

I find Aaron in his childhood bed, hiding beneath a pillow.

"They're so fucking mean," he sobs. From downstairs we hear the sounds of his parents doing the dishes. Aaron's bedroom has an instrument corner containing a mandolin, a guitar, and an accordion.

"I have to get out of here," he says.

"We'll get you out of here," I say, cradling him.

thirteen

With Aaron's last paycheck from the Greta Gerwig film, he takes me out to celebrate at Minetta Tavern. It's a Greenwich Village relic with red leather booths and chessboard tile, with caricatures of dead actors adorning the walls. We order two glasses of Bordeaux and steak frites, with a plate of bread doused in butter. I don't consider many things sacred, but in the ensuing weeks since leaving Seth, I have come to feel that my relationship with Aaron is sacred. We're standing at a pivotal intersection in both of our lives. It feels preordained that the stakes are low for both of us: neither of us has bad credit, college loans, or children to worry about, and that leaves this period of our lives free as a space of mutation and transformation. Ours may well become a legendary artistic collaboration. Patti Smith and Robert Mapplethorpe. Maya Deren and Alexander Hammid.

I envision myself becoming a softer, more introverted, more introspective, deeper, and more prolific person as Aaron's creative and romantic partner. I've wanted to be sensitive to Seth's feelings, so have deactivated my Facebook, Instagram, and Twitter accounts. I've told Aaron that in general I don't like having my picture taken, and I ask him not to post about us. Privately, I don't want to rub my new happiness in Seth's face. I want to insulate Aaron from the judgment and interference of people who think they know things about me.

My past mistakes should not reflect poorly on him. Aaron has done nothing wrong.

My phone rings and I wouldn't normally answer it at the table, but it seems Odessa is in crisis. This is the third day in a row she's called me, and people in our age group don't call. My work schedule, lack of privacy since moving into Leonard's, and poor reception on the subway have made it difficult for Odessa and me to talk, so I've kept our conversations brief. She asks me how I'm doing, and I say I'm processing, resting, and practicing self-care. She asks me how I'm spending my free time. This seems invasive, but I tell her I'm cocooning.

"Reading," I say. "Working on *True Love*."

"The script with Aaron?"

"Did I tell you about that?"

"You sent me his song."

"Right."

"What's going on with you two?"

"We've decided to approach the thriller writer about executive-producing."

"That's not what I asked you."

"I'm sorry, what are you asking?"

Aaron touches my shoulder, and I look up to see our waiter depositing two steaks on the table, pooling in blood. A man with a Polaroid camera exits the back room and begins circulating throughout the restaurant, taking people's pictures. Two tables down from us, a Midwestern father hands him a bill and his flashbulb discharges. He sets the photo facedown on the tablecloth.

"Don't treat me like a moron," says Odessa.

"We're looking at apartments together," I say. "It makes sense financially."

"Are you ready for that?"

"Are you okay?" says Aaron.

"Can I call you later?" I say.

"I need to tell you something," she says.

"What?"

"I'm pregnant."

The photographer reaches us and Aaron hands him a bill. The flash ignites and he sets the photo before me, emerging from the developer. My face is obscured by my phone's reflection.

ODESSA COMES TO New York the next week under the pretense of visiting her ex-stepfather, to tell him the news in person. She keeps in touch with Dennis because he sometimes gives her money, though her mother was only married to him for a year shortly after Odessa gave birth to Maxima. I have always wondered whether he and Odessa were sleeping together. I assume she's slept with most people. When she arrives at his Riverside Drive apartment, she calls me and says, "Dennis is drunk and on pills. We can't stay here." Her voice is muffled, like she's whispering in a closet. It's one in the morning, and I wonder for more than a moment whether this was her plan all along. Being drunk and on pills is not usually a deal-breaker for her. But what choice do I have now but to tell her to come to Leonard's? If Max weren't in the picture, I wouldn't, but I can't put a child out on the street. I've always felt protective of Max. I'm not a monster. I'm convinced that Odessa is psychic. She knew what poor timing this would be for me.

"I have to deal with this," I tell Aaron. I leave him in the daybed and sneak through the door into Leonard's room. His breathing is long and shallow. It had become necessary for me at a certain point to explain Aaron's presence to him. We'd overslept one morning and exited the closet-bedroom together. Leonard was in the kitchen. "This is Aaron," I said, standing there in my oversize T-shirt, with no pants on. "He's a friend. He lives on Staten Island, but he's working on a movie shooting nearby. They went late on set and he has to be back this morning. I hope that's okay."

I kneel at Leonard's bedside now and appeal to him, not as a friend but as a sworn guardian of security. "My sister is pregnant," I say. "Her baby's father is a violent felon." So he won't be concerned that Ian will come here, I add, "He's in Florida. She ran away from him and she thought she could stay with me. If she and my niece could just sleep in the living room for two nights, it would really help them out. Please."

ODESSA TAKES THE daybed, Max takes the sofa, and Aaron and I share a blanket on the floor. I call out of work the next morning saying I have a family emergency. I pass my duties on to an ambitious young bookseller with aspirations for a raise that will never come because she is female and too polite to ask for anything that isn't offered. This counts as one of my sick days, and I don't get paid if I'm not on the clock. I mention this fact to Odessa as I hang up the phone. I feel like the timing of her calamity is something she's doing to me personally. We sit on the fire escape and she lights a joint, explaining that it helps with her morning sickness. Leonard lives in the Hasidic neighborhood of Borough Park. All the windows have cages on them, large enough for infants to play inside, suspended above the sidewalks.

"I know you think I fucked up," she says, passing it to me. The sun cuts into my eyes. Leonard has left for work, and Aaron for his parents' house, and Max is still sleeping. Odessa has missed three periods and, looking at her, I foretell that she's about to ask me whether she should have an abortion.

"What would you do if you were me?"

I'm distraught. "Do what you think is best," I say. She'll do what she wants. Most likely she'll have Ian's baby. Odessa has always been afraid to rise to her true potential. I'll never forget when she told me what Mission had said to her: "Nina is right, Odessa. You could have gone so much further in life if you hadn't had a baby." I denied ever saying it. We were at a house party when she confronted me, and Max was eleven, waiting outside in the car. I felt like Mission had been paraphrasing and taking me out of context. I agreed with the sentiment. I just wouldn't have said it like that to her face.

"When did this start with Aaron?"

I stare at her blankly.

"Did you do it in Seth's bed?"

"Nope, never there."

"How do you think he would feel?"

"You know, I never really thought about that, Odessa. That's a really good question. You should ask him."

"Aaron is obviously in love with you."

"I'm in love with him."

"Are you, though?"

"Yes. Actually, we're getting married," I say, and I hope that this gives me power. I hope it justifies what is otherwise unjustifiable because love has no explanation and cannot be moralized. If I'm in a trance, I am not in control of myself; if I'm gesturing toward a higher purpose, sacrificing my self-respect for the greater good, then all is forgiven and understood. I see that Odessa views my condition as analogous to hers. I see that she wants to have Ian's baby and that, as with me, there is no rational reason.

"When did you decide this?"

"Just this week."

"Does Aaron know about Seth?"

"Shut up," I say.

She shuts up.

"Shut the fuck up," I say, "for once."

"God, Nina." She watches a Hasidic child exit the back door of his row house into a walled-in courtyard. "Are we going to spend any alone time with you while we're here, or is it all going to be with Aaron?"

"I didn't ask you to be here."

"Did it ever occur to you that I'm not only here for you?"

"Did it ever occur to you that I can't help you right now?"

WE TAKE OUR place in the Marriages/Deaths line at the Brooklyn courthouse. I wear a cream cotton dress I've had since high school, when I stole it from the Charlotte Russe in Tyrone Mall. It has tiny black flowers around the neckline, and it ties in the back with a big bow. Aaron is wearing dirty white Vans with black jeans and his father's collared shirt, with no tie. Max is scrolling on Instagram, and it's unclear whether they understand or Odessa has explained to them or they care about the gravity of what is happening. A large African family gathers behind us, dressed in sequins, and Odessa openly stares at them.

In my purse I'm carrying the wax-sealed bottle containing the vows I wrote with Aaron last night on the daybed, while Odessa, Max, and Leonard were watching *Blade Runner* in the living room. We sealed it with Crayolas and a Bic lighter, and after the ceremony, we'll leave Odessa and Max at the courthouse steps and walk to the middle of the Brooklyn Bridge to toss our promises into the East River, entrusting them to the infinite flow.

I vow to support you.

I vow to respect you.

I vow to protect you.

I vow to listen.

I vow never to lie to you.

On the metal chairs where we wait, Odessa tells me that Jared is now monogamous with Sofia. I can't imagine what conversation needed to happen for him to agree to it. I think back to that night on his couch when he laid his head in my lap. I thought then maybe it would happen between us. I'm anxious I'm being deceptive even in harboring this memory. There's a feeling that surrounds this state of mind that I didn't create and can't control, an overwhelming hunger driving me in search of blood, an emotion that dilates, that I might see more clearly through obscurity. "They fucked in the back of Claudette's car on the shoulder of I-4," says Odessa. "Then Sofia read his texts and found out he was fucking like seven other women. He texted Claudette saying, 'There's an email coming for you and you're not gonna like it.' The email was telling her not to interfere in his relationship anymore, and not to contact him again. Claudette thinks Sofia made him send it."

"Jared isn't monogamous," I say.

"He says he is," says Odessa. "And Claudette is asexual now."

They call our number, and the four of us approach the Plexiglas window. I learn while filling out our marriage application that Aaron is a Leo. An inexplicable change occurs on the courthouse's cheap plastic dais when I look into his face and know that he is forevermore my husband. I am younger and older than I've ever been. I am sinking into a new dimension of joint selfhood. I make myself a clean and perfect creature, the most perfect, selfless creature.

fourteen

I ask my parents to Skype with me, saying that I need to tell them something important. I give them no further information. My gut tells me that my mother will make time for drama. In my text I apologize that it's hard for her, with her schedule. I explain that I know she's been in the area lately, helping Nana move into a new nursing home.

It's the first time I've seen either of my parents' faces in months, and the first time in years that I've seen them in the same room. The sight of them side by side is jarring. For a second I feel like I'm twelve. They've convened at my father's house, sitting at the island counter. Aaron is next to me on the daybed at Leonard's. My parents examine him.

I show them my ring, which we bought for twenty-five dollars at a prop store near Port Authority bus station. I'd wanted a ring that belonged to a dead woman. I'd wanted it to have a patina. The old woman who sold it to me had worked out of the third floor of the warehouse building since the seventies. She'd filled it with antiques and cobwebbed furniture that she rented out to theaters.

I followed her through the dusty pathways to a carved chiffonier with glass doors from which she extracted a thin gold band with no diamond. It was engraved with *June 9, 1915*. Exactly one hundred years prior to that moment. It wasn't possible to see this as anything other than a sign from the universe. Aaron's ring was cheap, from Chinatown. A simple, unbroken silver.

I thought telling the story would add levity to the reality that we could not afford proper rings, that I could not get married like a regular person.

"We wanted privacy," I tell my parents, almost adding that it isn't personal.

We sit in silence until my mother says, "It makes me wonder what else you haven't told us."

"I've barely talked to you in months," says my father. "You never answer the phone."

"That's not true."

"Yes, it is," says my mother. "Who is this person? Excuse me," she says to Aaron.

"My friend Aaron."

"Your friend?"

"The one I wrote *True Love* with."

"You wrote what?"

"The movie."

She thinks about this. She leans in to whisper something to my father. He shakes his head at the Formica counter. "You didn't tell us about that."

"Yes, I did."

Aaron reaches for my hand. It's embarrassing to touch him in front of my parents. I pull away.

"Did you know it was my birthday yesterday?" says my mother.

"I'm sorry."

I'm not good at remembering birthdays. I'm not good at remembering people. I'm not good at keeping in touch with people on the phone. I'm not good at carrying on an enthusiastic conversation. I'm not good at ignoring what else is happening in a room. I'm not good at being vulnerable in the presence of third parties. I'm not comfortable with the silence between speech.

"I feel like you don't even care."

"We're not mad at you, Nina," says my father. "We just wish we could have been there."

"I look forward to meeting you both," says Aaron.

I EMAIL THEM all the following week from his parents' house. We've gone there to retrieve my boxes. We've convinced a landlord to invest in us as newlyweds, and tomorrow we plan to celebrate together in a café in our new neighborhood of Kensington, Brooklyn. We enjoy Kensington for its comically Anglophile name, especially considering the majority of our neighbors are South Asian. We are part of the southward creep of gentrification. We have a locally famous hummus restaurant around the corner on a main street of brunch cafés, coffee shops, and a food co-op.

Mom and Dad, you've expressed that you're in shock because you don't know Aaron that well, I say, writing on my phone in his parents' guest bathroom. They recently remodeled it in lavender. *This is understandable. We mentioned that we went to school together. Aaron roomed with a good friend of mine. We had other mutual friends, but weren't close until years later, when we became pen pals. This was around the time of* Numina. *In fact, Aaron has a story in the issue I edited—feel free to revisit the copy I sent you. The story is quite good, if incomplete, but that was sort of the idea. Dad, Aaron has worked on commercials. You have this in common. You're both extremely convincing. Mom, Aaron's mom is a teacher, 2nd grade next year. You'll be happy to learn that his family votes Democrat. Aaron is a year and a half younger than I am. That said, he's a man, not a boy. He treats me like an adult with a mind of my own. This is much appreciated. He gives me plenty of space. He's smart. He's funny. He's also hand-some, isn't he? He's nice to me and everyone else, and has friends of his own. Everyone who meets him likes him immediately. I'm sure he's happy to answer any questions you may have. Aaron, do you have any questions for my parents? Reply-all. Love, Nina.*

I leave the bathroom and look for Aaron. I told him I did not want to spend the night here after the way his mother reacted to our elopement, but the dessert portion of the dinner ended hours ago. When we told her we were married over the phone, she screamed at us for almost an hour. Sitting next to me in his car, Aaron held her up between us on speaker so that we could jointly pacify her. She demanded to know why smart people would do something so stupid. "You need a job to find an apartment to live like married people. Or did you think you would still live with us?" she said. I apologized and begged her not to be angry. I told her I liked and respected her. We later learned she'd discovered earlier that day that Aaron's younger brother, who still lives at home, had tattooed a paragraph of blended, unattributed platitudes by dead white men on his calf. She saw it when he walked to the bathroom that morning in his briefs. Hearing how distraught she was, Aaron rushed in to save her, allowing her to shift the focus of her hysterics to his own betrayal, receiving the blows of her anger, and responding with remorse and reassurance. Of course he still loves her; we both do. Let him prove that he won't disappoint her. She ended up cosigning our lease. She paid Aaron's half of the rent and deposit.

I find them together now in the basement, where they're elbow-deep in a storage bin of Aaron's old homework. She hands me a typed school report he wrote in the eighth grade, about planetary moons. It's bound with brads and a plastic sheet protector over a cover he drew himself, depicting a boy looking through a telescope with his father. *Copernicus was thought insane during his time for claiming that the Sun was at the center of our universe,* the report reads. *It was Galileo's observation of the phases of Venus that finally proved the heliocentric theory.*

"This is pretty advanced for an eighth grader," I say, trying to sound impressed.

"He may have had some help." His mother winks.

Aaron clicks his tongue.

"What?" she asks.

"Why do you have to do that?"

She looks at me. "What did I say?"

"You always find some little way to cut me down."

"You probably had some help, that's all I said. Is that wrong?"

"Can't you let me feel good about something?"

"I'm sorry, I didn't mean to hurt your feelings. He's very sensitive," she says to me.

Aaron's face is red, a vein bisecting it.

"Sorry," she says to him. Then, to me, "Aaron was in the gifted program."

WE BRING MY boxes to the Kensington studio. It's four hundred square feet on the ground floor, with no central circulation, so the windows must remain open at all times, even while we're sleeping, despite the fact it faces the street. Our bedroom is also the living room, which connects to the kitchen and a narrow hallway to the bathroom. Our two windows look out on the building's entrance. In the morning, the caretaker of our elderly neighbor parks the woman on the porch to sun. An ornery Albanian man chain-smokes and spits gray phlegm onto the worn garnet steps. From the nursing home down the block, each passing van and ambulance kicks up dust that settles in a film on our curb furniture. In the evening, children run up and down the block and onto the gated grass beneath us. Before dawn, the drug dealer from the third floor screams at his girlfriend and throws her clothes onto the fire escape.

My terror and euphoria in the early days of our marriage come from my certainty that Aaron loves me. "I'm not used to this," I tell him. We're in the stage of our love's deepening through rejoicing that I have left another man to be with him.

"I stole you away from Seth," he says, lifting my shirt. He enjoys tarnishing Seth's memory while he fucks me. Seth was afraid it would go to my head if I were allowed to think too highly of myself, so he would subtly remind me that I was shallow and narcissistic. With him it was expected that a humble genius would go for days, weeks even, without bathing, or years wearing the same threadbare Jawbreaker T-shirt.

Aaron's features are delicate, almost feminine. His fragility pleads with me, compels me to protect him by telling him that I can't be enough for him. "I've had years of negative conditioning," I say. "Every time I look at you, you're looking at me and it scares me. Seth never looked at me."

When Aaron wants to praise me, I ask him to please say anything else. "Instead of telling me I'm beautiful, ask me what book I'm reading, or bring up something that happened in the news," I say. I worry that Aaron is placing me on a pedestal, that he will be disappointed when he realizes I'm not who he thought I was. He'll think I've deceived him, though I tried to warn him about how I am.

THE NIGHT BEFORE going to the courthouse with Aaron, I woke up crying on Leonard's daybed. We were soaked in my sweat. I watched a dream recede, this one recurring, based on one of my earliest memories. In it I am three, crouched in the early morning light of my bedroom. I'm throwing my seashell collection—gathered on repeat pilgrimages to the beach with my family—one by one into my closet, which Jung might call a symbol. I've plucked these shells from the sand at the edge of the water with my own fingers. I believe that if I toss the right seashell into my closet, it will make a rainbow I can ride away from everything around me. Already, by age three, I feel aware of the existence of evil. Perhaps I intuited it from the beginning, the closing-off of possibilities starting in the moment the egg of me was fertilized; and my expectations were reified by culture as I matured. My mother cuts the yellow light of the hallway as she looks in on me tossing the last shell. No rainbow appears.

Aaron was still sleeping beside me. I imagined sharing this dream with him, then realized I couldn't. "My dreams are frustrating," he'd told me. "I'm always doing something annoying, like digging a staple out of a stack of paper, or typing a message that's melting." I'd come to understand that Aaron believed his mind was trolling him. He saw nothing meaningful or illuminating in his dreams. He'd never wake in the morning and say to me, "I had the strangest dream," and close his eyes to recount it. He'd never wake crying from a dream and ask me to hold him. Dreaming only served to remind Aaron that he was powerless.

I watched his eyelids flutter. They were translucent like baby birds. I shook him. "I can't marry you," I said, sitting up. "I haven't been single in years. You don't know me. I'll ruin you."

He was silent.

"This is reckless and stupid," I said. "I'll be trapped. I'll never have my own space. I'll never be able to pick up and travel. I'll have to tell you about all my plans. I'll never do anything without you.

Our lives will become enmeshed. How will I know who I am any-more separate from you? You'll think you own me."

He pulled me down and rolled on top of me. I was sobbing. I was grieving everything I'd lost and all I'd never have and all I stood to lose. I was sickened by my credulity; I had no reason to trust Aaron. I hadn't even told my parents about us, too afraid of their disap-proval. I hated myself. I was dangerously projecting my desires onto Aaron. So naive. So foolish. So trapped.

"I don't want to control you," Aaron said, and I felt myself falling back. "I don't want to own you. I don't want to keep you from doing whatever you need to do. I just want to love you. I just want to make things with you, and make love to you, and laugh with you. If you don't want that, you can leave me."

He swore it.

I TRAIN MYSELF to love him in a married way. I willingly enter a feed-back loop of obsession, hoping my love for Aaron and his for me will protect me from myself. I ask Aaron for daily reminders: "Do you still love me?" I begin to think that everything we do is an act of love or a cry for love. "You have the most stunning mouth," he tells me; it feels like he's hypnotizing me to control me, and I happily abandon myself to him. He holds his hands to my cheeks and looks into me. He does this while I'm eating tacos, brushing my teeth, waiting at the pharmacy. The note of wonder in his voice makes me aware of how seldom I feel impelled to remark on his appearance, so I look for features to notice and call out to him as my favorites. "The mole on your left cheek," I say. "The craters of your hazel eyes. The tiny bald spot on your temple." I describe them for him. I believe what I say to him.

We make weekly trips to the co-op together to stock up on the few vegetables and fruits Aaron is not allergic to. As a housewarming present, his mother took me on a personal tour of our local produce section, to school me in his dietary triggers. Foods he can't tolerate include drupes and nightshades, peppers, eggplants, peaches, plums, avocados, any raw vegetable, chilies, huckleberries, cherries, and cinnamon. We can't have cats. We can only have a hypoallergenic dog, like a Maltese.

AARON AND I are in the produce section procuring ingredients for tonight's puttanesca and *Taxi Driver* and chill. I almost don't recognize Daniel at the next bin over examining a peach—he's so groomed and apparently sober. His dimples give him away when he smiles and says something to the person beside him. I recognize that person as my college suitemate, Heidi. She's holding a bag of peaches as if selling them on QVC. When we lived together, I used to taunt her for her wholesomeness, her honors classes, her handheld Dirt Devil, her pore strips. Her clean presentation made me feel freakish. I thought if she hated herself a little bit, it might make her more tolerable.

I reached out to her before moving back to the city and apologized for the way I'd behaved when we lived together. I explained that I was in a very dark place at the time, and had moved past it. I thanked her for having the courage to show me who I was when I was using—I actually used the word "using." I asked if she'd be open to getting coffee when I was back in the city, hoping she'd hook me up with some work, but she never responded. Now she's grocery shopping with Daniel, a participant in the dark history that necessitated my atonement to her.

Their heads turn in unison. From the looks on everyone's faces

I can see us all simultaneously remember the night at a party when I fucked Daniel on a balcony. Daniel was about to leave on his first tour, and everyone wanted to fuck him. I handed him an American Spirit as he leaned against a banister ten floors above the East Village. "I'm not done with you, you know," he said.

Inside, people were doing keg stands and playing beer pong. They sounded miles away. I thought of how far Daniel and I had come in four years alongside each other. I was a semester away from graduating with my degree in English: useless, yet versatile in theory. I had barely made it there, and I wouldn't make it to the end, but I didn't know that yet. I was ovulating and had been doing lines since ten in the morning.

"What do you have to finish with me?" I said.

He reached for my neck and closed his hand around it. He leaned in. Our tongues laced together. I knew he was using me, but I wanted him to possess me. I wanted him to punch me as I was riding his dick and say, "Nina, I love you. Stop living like this."

People gathered around us. Someone started chanting. We fell to the floor, and suddenly Daniel was inside me. I screamed his name. I blacked out, and when I opened my eyes again, Heidi was looking down on me.

There is no escape route in the supermarket. Daniel is smiling at Aaron. "Hey, buddy," he says, and they hug. Aaron pulls away. Daniel looks at him, then at me. "Good to see you," he says. "Nina."

"Hey, Daniel," I say. I wonder if he read the email I sent to Heidi. Surely they've talked about me. I assume they decided together that she shouldn't respond. Rumors circulated after my disappearance from school. One said I had tried to kill myself. One said I had run away with a heroin addict.

"Do you live in the neighborhood?" asks Daniel.

"We just moved here," says Aaron.

"Both of you?"

Aaron laughs. He looks at me. I'm expected to say something.

"We're married," I say.

"Wow," Daniel says. "Congratulations. I didn't know you guys were dating."

I smile at Heidi. She looks at the floor.

"Are you still making music?" says Aaron.

"I don't know if you heard what happened with Tree Service. We're on an indefinite hiatus."

"I'm sorry."

"It's for the best, actually. I'm doing solo stuff now. Come over sometime, I'll play it for you."

"Yeah, we'll have to get together."

THE NIGHT IS balmy when we finally escape.

"He's cleaned up a lot," Aaron says, stepping around a dog tied to a parking meter. We turn down a brick street to get off the main thoroughfare, into a part of the neighborhood composed of mansions with lawns and broad sidewalks with flowering trees. We stop to admire a slow-moving bee, one of the year's last to die off.

"We all have," I say.

"He looks less like a tweaker."

"So do I."

"Honestly, I wouldn't be surprised if that's why the band broke up," he says.

We walk on and pass an elementary school, then a neighborhood library. I imagine that this would be a nice area to raise a family. I imagine that's why Daniel and Heidi live here.

"Touring probably made it worse," he says. "And women."

My phone vibrates. I take it out of my pocket, hidden by a grocery bag. **Is it true?** Brian texts. I put it back.

"Makes sense he would end up with Heidi. She's so stable," I say.

"She's exactly the same."

My phone vibrates. **Are you married?**

fifteen

It's been a year since Aaron and I began writing *True Love*. We've rewritten it five or six times. We've recently added a subplot loosely based on Aaron's falling-out with Daniel right after Tree Service released their first EP. It shows the tremendous sense of loss Aaron felt when he realized that Daniel wasn't a person he knew anymore. During the years Daniel was touring, he'd become someone Aaron could no longer talk to—scrawny and pompous and unconcerned with anything that wasn't pussy, drugs, or upward mobility, according to Aaron. But knowing Aaron, I find it hard not to draw conclusions of my own about their friendship's breakdown. Each time I think we're close to finishing the script, he finds something wrong with it. "It's not calibrated correctly," he says. He asks me for ideas, then shoots them all down. I don't believe Aaron wants to resolve the issue with Daniel. Conflict gives his life meaning.

When I was living at Leonard's, Aaron and I corresponded daily about the script, and our physical separation allowed us to generate content while Gchatting, texting, emailing, without stopping to fuck, clean the kitchen, watch *Sopranos* reruns, or go to the bar. I wanted to harness the productivity of the Leonard period and carry it into a new life, a better me, but I'm beginning to think that's not going to happen. Our studio is nothing like the live/work space I'd envisioned. The script has sat largely untouched for three months. The movie's ending is still uncertain. The story as we originally conceived of it has proven unrealistic. There's too little separation between *True Love* and the rest of life.

I'M STANDING IN Brian's bedroom. Wetness runs down the insides of my legs as if I've just urinated. A puddle forms around my feet. My shorts and panties lie on the floor next to me. I look around, noticing my surroundings as Brian steps away from me. There's only a mattress and Brian, who points to it and tells me to lie down.

"Have you talked to him?" asks Aaron, looking at me over his shoulder.

"Not in months."

He pauses the video on his computer. "Are you sure about that?"

"Yes."

He hits the space bar. Brian kneels. He kisses my neck and my breasts. His ass is small and flat. His crotch presses into me.

"We don't talk," I say. "I swear."

"I saw his name on your phone."

"When?"

I take off my shirt and lie down. Brian brings his dick to my mouth.

"When we were walking back from the co-op."

"I didn't answer him."

Aaron looks at me. He's crying.

"I didn't, Aaron, I swear to God. I have nothing to say to him."

"Why pretend he hadn't texted you?"

"I forgot."

"That seems unlikely."

"I have no desire to be in contact with him. I don't even want to think about him. He's clearly a predator. He's the white Bill Cosby."

"Show me your phone."

"No." The video plays on. I hit the space bar and freeze on Brian's fingers bent like a fishhook in my mouth.

"If you didn't answer him, then you have nothing to hide."

"I'm not hiding anything, I just don't want to set a precedent for you having access to my phone."

He hits the space bar.

"Stop it." I reach for the laptop, but Aaron blocks me. I close my eyes and listen to myself gagging on Brian's cock. I start to cry but suppress it. Aaron hits the space bar and looks at me.

"Why did he send me this?"

"We don't even know he did," I say. "I don't recognize that email address."

"Who else would have?"

"I don't know," I say. "I didn't even know it existed."

"Are you upset?" he says. He points to the time stamp. "This was while you were with Seth."

"Yeah, you knew that."

"You told me you were in love with Brian. Are you still in love with him?"

"I thought I was at the time, but I'm not."

His knee begins shaking. I think it will fly off his body. I put my hand on it.

"Show me your phone," he says. He reaches for my hand. I pull away from him. "Just show me the conversation."

"Absolutely not."

"Let me see it."

"No."

"Just show it to me."

He lunges at me. I jump up and run to the bathroom. He follows and I try to close the door, but he pushes against it. I push back. "Aaron, stop!" I yell. He doesn't. "Stop it!" I throw my weight against the door and it slams shut. I lock it and Aaron hammers on the outside. He kicks it several times with the full force of his leg, and I sit with my back against it and feel the blows. The wall beside me crumbles inside itself. I text him, **Please stop!!!** I bang on the door. "Stop it!" I scream. I scream as loud as I can, an open vowel, enough for the neighbors on either side of us and above to hear. I punch the door several times and the banging stops. Three dots appear in our text conversation. They disappear.

He pounds on the door with his fist. "I'm not texting with you on the other side of the *fucking* door," he says. He punches with each word.

"Leave me alone!" I say.

Bang-bang-bang-bang.

"I'M GOOD," I tell Odessa. Our conversations are infrequent, and when we talk, I'm always trying to get off the phone with her. I'm always afraid when she phones that the call will last half an hour, and I never have half an hour to spare. When I'm not at work, I'm writing with my phone on silent, or I'm uploading short stories to Submittable so they can be ignored for three months, then rejected, or I'm spending time with Aaron, since he often complains that I'm neglecting him. I'm doing my best to be a "good wife." We've neatly compartmentalized our Brian disagreement. I've promised that I'm not the cheating type anymore and have tried to force the idea into myself. I tell myself I was driven by circumstances to act out of character in the past, as a form of protection, as a way to keep something of my life just for me, to breathe when I felt I was suffocating. We've taken up a new hobby of cooking together. He calls me his sous chef and his "wifey for life-y." I feel obligated to answer the phone one out of every three times Odessa calls now, if I can, if I don't have oven mitts on my hands. Just enough to avoid the appearance of avoiding her. I can hear in her pinched tone that our conversations fall short of what she wants. Aaron is always in the room with me, or in the next room listening through the door.

"I've been working a lot," I tell her. I try to sound overwhelmed so she feels badly for taking up my time. I sometimes walk around the block if I need privacy, but it's late October now and sleeting. I've been in my pajamas all day, cleaning our hovel, since Aaron infrequently sweeps or Swiffers or makes the bed. I lean against the locked door of the bathroom and keep my voice low.

"Can you talk?" she asks.

"For a minute."

"I want you to be with me for the birth of my child." She's due in six weeks. "You're the closest person in the world to me besides my grandma. You're like my sister, Nina. Please."

"I don't have the money to fly to Florida, Odessa. I'm so sorry. I can't afford time off."

"Please, Nina. Don't tell me you can't."

"Aaron isn't working. It's the slow season for him. And it's the holiday season for me so the bookstore is really busy, plus I'll be in school."

"Nina, I'm scared. I don't want Ian on her birth certificate. I had a strong intuition about him and I went to see my psychic and she told me that he has a lot of negative energy right now. I'm thinking of having the baby somewhere else so he can't be with me. I think he might be losing his mind."

"Is it possible you're just scared about having the baby?"

"I don't think so."

"Somewhere else like where?"

"Like New York, maybe."

"New York?"

"Do you think I could stay with you?"

I imagine Odessa sleeping on the love seat. Our love seat designates the living room portion of our apartment. It's within spitting distance of the bed. Making a bed for her baby in the bathtub. Max on the floor. "Odessa, we don't have any extra room. We don't even have a full-on sofa. We can't have you, Max, and a newborn in here. This isn't a tenement house."

"Then come be with me."

"I can't, okay?" I'm yelling. "I shouldn't have to say it like this."

"I understand."

"I'm so sorry," I say, quieter. "Can you stay with Dennis? He owns his apartment. You know he would let you."

She's silent, thinking about it. Aaron is nailing something into the wall of our kitchen. I bet it's something super imaginative, like an old license plate.

"Yeah, maybe," she says.

AS THE WEATHER turns colder, Aaron begins smoking more inside. He doesn't ask if he can; he sees me going outside to smoke and stays where he always is—in his metal folding chair positioned before his metal desk by the window. The desk is an imposing midcentury factory piece painted slate gray and rusting. He bought it on Craigslist for a hundred dollars. He didn't tell me he was buying it; he decided one day while I was at work that having a "designated work space" of his own was more important than pitching in for the gas and electricity bills. I came home and the desk was here, taking up an entire corner. He leaves the window cracked just enough for the smoke to travel back into the room on a jet stream.

I close the door on the bathroom, and the air smells cleaner. I try to read or write silently against the toilet, but the sounds of Aaron's movie, Aaron arguing on the phone with his mother, clanging pots, making dinner, travels through the cheap plywood door. When he needs to shit, he barges in, sits on the toilet, and says, "You don't have to leave, don't worry." He shits and makes grunting noises while I try to read. Sometimes he comes in just to tell me he loves me. "I haven't seen you for hours," he says. He tries to kiss me.

I work forty hours a week for an annual income of $25,000. Aaron is paid a hundred dollars a day for occasional three-week gigs of twelve-hour workdays on movie sets. These come along through his personal connections, which I've learned are few. Every other week, he asks his parents to buy us groceries. Instead of sending us money, they drive to our neighborhood and take us to the grocery store. Walking through the aisles, his mother and I talk about Aaron's favorite foods and his sensitivities. Gathering in our studio after, they make suggestions for income streams he hasn't considered. He could get a job apprenticing for a photographer. It should be easy since he has experience with cameras, they say. As a bystander to these sessions, I'm at once parent, child, and wife. The various responsibilities of these roles carry into my everyday life as Aaron's partner. **Why hasn't Aaron paid his parking ticket?** his mother texts me. Yes, she knows he hasn't paid it, she says—though I didn't—because his father owns the car's registration.

I begin to note that Aaron is depressive. I start awake in the middle of the night, and he's smoking out the window with his back to me, playing *SimCity* on his vintage laptop computer. He never goes to bed when I do anymore. He'll stay up for hours click-click-clicking his broken touch pad next to my head. He can't take his laptop into another room because he can't unplug it from the wall anymore since the battery is dead, and he is too proud to ask his parents to buy him a new one, and too lazy to restart the computer were he to move it into the kitchen. Though his parents pay for almost everything he needs, it's essential that he rarely ask them to pay for things to preserve his ego. They assume he needs underwear, laundry detergent, Swiffers, and they ship those things to our apartment via Amazon. "My mother makes me feel guilty," he says, unpacking another box of paper towels. He can't bear to give her another reason to criticize him, something new to use against him. I lie in the dark watching him light one cigarette off another. I've told him that I hate it when he smokes inside, so now he waits until I'm asleep.

I ATTEMPT TO talk to Aaron about money. I've identified money as the veil for his primary fear, which is failure, and beneath failure, rejection, and beneath rejection, uselessness. That I'm the primary breadwinner in our household emasculates him, makes him, by masculine standards, "useless," a label he uses often, and which he learned from his father, who aims it at people like an inconveniently placed homeless person panhandling outside the supermarket, or the inattentive waiter at Le Pain Quotidien, or his wife's extended family, from whom they are all estranged. To be useless is to have failed to earn or ceded your privilege to take up space on this planet. To him the useless are born fundamentally unintelligent, or have become stupid through some fault of their own—many "useless" people are also "stupid." An inability to earn money is at the core of uselessness. What they've done or failed to do has rendered them forevermore unworthy of money, and thereby deserving to be discarded:

trash. Money is Aaron's primary system of valuation. Being poor is the foundation and evidence of uselessness.

Since he doesn't make money, Aaron is cheap. When he buys people presents, he makes a point of telling them how little he paid for them. When I leave the bathroom light on, he scolds me.

Lately Aaron has been interning for an indie production collective whose mumblecore horror feature won the Sundance Grand Jury Prize last year. That he's an intern makes it possible for the bros at the collective to pay him only occasionally. Their deal is a handshake. They dangle the carrot that they might one day produce Aaron's script if he sucks their dicks enough now. They ghost him, then invite him to exclusive screenings at MoMA, or New Year's parties in the Village, then send him home from set for "behaving erratically," then take him out for day drinks in Williamsburg. They hold his measly paychecks because "Anthony was doing blow last night and he's not awake yet," and the bank closes in an hour on Saturday. I've returned to modeling for drawing classes for an extra hundred dollars a week, since even with Aaron's parents' contributions, we can't afford rent and utilities on my bookstore income alone.

"Can't you find a part-time job in a coffee shop?" I say.

"I need to be available in case they ask me to work on a movie," says Aaron. We're finding a table at our neighborhood brunch café. It's Sunday morning and we woke up late and cuddled in a sunbeam, then discovered we didn't have any food in the house. We felt too lazy to walk to the corner store and then walk home and cook. We act like we deserve to treat ourselves.

"That's the thing about coffee shops," I say. "Your hours are flexible."

"I don't have any experience as a barista."

"Surely they would train you."

"They wouldn't even hire me. My résumé doesn't show that I have any coffee shop experience."

"The people at Qathra know you. You're there every day."

The waiter comes to take our drink order. I order coffee and water. Aaron orders an Americano.

"I don't want to work in a coffee shop," he says. "It's degrading."

"Please tell me you're joking."

"It's not what I need to be doing."

"Your job is not your whole identity."

"I need to be working on my script. Ben gave me notes and I need to get him a new draft by next month."

"You can work on it in off-hours and on the weekends, like everyone else. Including me."

"Working in a coffee shop would be a waste of my time. I could use that time writing."

"Then they need to pay you when they say they're going to pay you, and they need to pay you more." I watch the waiter as he finishes making our coffees behind the bar. He pours chilled half-and-half into a shared decanter and walks it all over to our table. We order different dishes both featuring poached eggs. Mine comes with apricot rose preserves on an English muffin. As the waiter departs, Aaron points out that my order was slightly more expensive than his.

"Please don't criticize my order."

"You say you're worried about money. Then what are we doing here?"

"I'm telling you that I can't support both of us."

"I need them to give me commercial work."

"That would be great."

"All I need is one person to take a chance on me."

"I'm taking a chance on you."

"Once I make this movie, everything will be easier."

"Hope so."

"You don't have to convince a million people to believe in you and give you money before you can write anything."

"You think it's easier for me? Nobody pays me for what I do. I work retail five fucking days a week and take my clothes off on the side."

"That's a little dramatic."

"That's literally what I do."

"Nobody pays me for what I do, either."

"That's not true, you just don't do enough of it. You sit around on your computer all day in a Wikipedia wormhole. Your computer doesn't even work. What can anyone give you to do on it?"

"Can you not yell? We're in public."

"Shut the fuck up, Aaron. You're so fucking entitled."

"Don't get your panties in a twist. I'm doing the best I can. It's hard for me to find work in my field."

"You're a college-educated white man."

"What does that mean?"

"You can do whatever the fuck you want."

"That's not true."

I go outside to smoke. I make a big show of storming out and bringing my coffee with me. The coffee is bitter. I sit on the partial wall of the restaurant's patio. The sky never lifted today, is a heavy, laughing charcoal. When I return to the table, Aaron has deposited his salad onto my plate. He can eat leafy greens but chooses not to, just to be safe. He's been waiting for me to return before he starts eating. He wants me to see how polite he is.

"All I'm saying is, there are ways we can save money until things pick up for me," he says.

"Are you going to tell me again that I'm not being frugal enough at the supermarket?"

"You bring home a new book every day."

"I get them for free."

"All of them?"

"Most."

"Do you really need the ones you're buying?"

"I get a forty percent staff discount."

"That's not what I asked."

"It's none of your business how I spend my own money."

"We need to be able to talk about this. I know it's hard, but please don't get defensive."

"I'm divorcing you if we're evicted. Let's talk about that."

"Don't joke like that," he says. "It's not nice."

He saves one of his eggs for later. He boxes it like a sacrifice.

sixteen

I begin seeing a West Village psychoanalyst who takes my insurance. I'm in the last semester of my MFA program; my thesis is a monstrous, mixed-genre novel about my mother that incorporates long sections of blackout poetry from the pages of *More Than Two* and *The Ethical Slut*. I've chewed off all of my cuticles trying to write it. It reveals perhaps too much about my mother, so I experiment with interleaving a fictional transcript of the black box recording of Admiral Richard E. Byrd's last transmission from his flight into the Hollow Earth. In it he encounters the Agharthans and is tasked with bringing back the message that the human race is headed for extinction. No one believes him. My hands and feet are the casualties. I wear bandages on my fingers, always in pain while I'm typing. I lie on the analyst's couch.

"They're never not bleeding," I say. "Not just my fingers, my toenails, too. I chew my toes and peel the skin, and there are open, bleeding sores on my hands and feet. Sometimes I eat the skin and the fingernails. It hurts to do the dishes. I'm embarrassed to hand people change at the bookstore. My fingers are covered in Band-Aids that I have to change whenever I shower. It hurts to wash my hair. Sometimes I don't even know that I'm bleeding, but even when I realize, it doesn't matter, I can't stop. My toes keep getting infected and keeping me up at night. I can't walk around the city."

"Why do you want to be in pain?" he asks, gentle and serious.

"You think I want this?"

"Do you?"

I consider it. "I guess it feels like I'm releasing something under pressure."

"What are you releasing?"

"Rage."

I visit the analyst every Thursday. I'm the last patient in the center before it closes. When I ask him how he's been since our last session, he says, "Well enough." He's in his mid-forties, tall and broad, Mediterranean, and impeccably dressed in a three-piece suit and leather shoes, with matching watch and socks. The sound of his white noise machine lulls me into a trance. We address each other by our last names. This lends our meetings a formality that fosters mutual fascination, to my mind. When I ask him what we should talk about, he tells me that he will "hold me to saying everything." It's what I've always wanted someone to say to me. I feel as if he already knows and accepts me.

For most of our sessions, the analyst says nothing. He allows me to talk. I worry at times that I'm boring him. I confess, "My husband is a very anxious man. We argue several times a week. Our arguments escalate and they last for hours, sometimes all night. We slam doors and scream at each other. He breaks furniture. He broke three tables in one month, so now we have a glass table, to discourage him from slamming things into it. It's like we're collaborating to control his temper. I try to physically separate myself from him to end the arguments, but he follows me around the tiny apartment, and there's nowhere for me to go. He tries to force me to talk to him. This morning, I closed the door on my office"—the small hallway between the kitchen and the bathroom, in which Aaron has removed the door of the utility closet and wedged a TV dinner tray inside with a folding chair—"and all morning, he yelled headlines at me from the next room while I was trying to write. 'Trump lost the Iowa caucuses.' 'The FBI is investigating the Flint water crisis.' Like he's Walter fucking Cronkite. I didn't have time to care about the fucking news. I had to leave the house at eleven to make my shift by noon. Then he decided he needed to water the plants in the bathtub. Three times. Each time he acknowledged that he was disrupting me. We talked about this less than a week ago. I had to run away to the library. It was full of babies and stay-at-home moms. Aaron opened the door all self-righteously when I came back to drop off my laptop. He says things he knows are wrong to manipulate me into reacting. He says the most horrible things to me. He asks me how long I need to be alone. If I say half an hour, I can hear him outside the bathroom door after twenty-nine minutes. I fantasize about crawling out the window instead of opening the door for him. The last time he did this, I cut myself."

I pull up my sleeve. There are three fresh gashes, half an inch wide and two inches long, across the middle of my forearm. The analyst doesn't say anything.

"I started cutting myself in the second grade, but I haven't done it since high school," I lie. "So, I consider this a sort of relapse."

I wait for him to respond, but he doesn't.

"Are you awake?" I say.

"Yes."

"Now he uses this as another excuse to never leave me alone. If I try to lock myself in the bathroom, he forces his way inside and makes a big show of fishing my razors out from under the sink. He's just trying to humiliate me. It's like he thinks he's my keeper. It's infantilizing. I feel like a captive animal. I don't know what to do."

"What comes to mind?" he says.

Divorce him, I think, but I say, "I'd like to find another way to handle my stress."

"Keep talking."

"We'd been arguing for three days when I did it. He drives me insane. He's angry and self-loathing, yelling at me, criticizing me. He micromanages even the way I make eggs. It's almost nonstop with brief intermissions of sweetness and apologizing. He tells me he loves me, then the smallest thing sets him off again. I cut myself in the bathroom and felt better afterward. What's wrong with that? We were finally able to go to sleep. The next morning, when he noticed the bloody tissue in the trash can, he started yelling again, accusing me of doing it to hurt him. How narcissistic can you be?"

I'd escaped into the rain and gone running down the street, hiding beneath awning after awning through Little Bangladesh. I reached the corner dive bar and spotted Daniel through the window, drinking alone. He looked up at me and we smiled, and I thought about going inside, but it was nine in the morning, and I didn't know why he would be there. I decided I didn't want to know.

"I went for a walk, and when I got back, the same argument started up again, from the night before. He can see in my face that I'm still upset. Even if I don't want to talk about it, or deny being upset, he can't be convinced otherwise. He needles me until I tell him what's bothering me. Sometimes I lie and say that I'm upset even when I'm not because I know it's what he wants to hear. Why does he want to hear that something's upsetting me? Why does he think something is wrong all the time? Who taught him this? And of course, it's his mother. All she does is complain. We stayed over at their house a few weeks ago and I woke up at eight o'clock on a Sunday morning to the sound of her screaming at Aaron's brother. He was still in bed, under the covers."

"Why was she screaming?"

"Because he got into Oxycontin and failed out of college in his first semester and then slept through his NA meeting. But he's some kind of genius. He can very quickly become an expert in anything. He figured out how to get onto the dark web and was all over Silk Road buying chemicals he and his friends mixed into drugs. I think they did something funny to his brain. He's not the same person he was six months ago."

I stumble on a memory of waking up in the Den of Inquiry, staring into a hole in my ceiling. A pipe had burst in the room above me, and I'd been sleeping in a pool of dirty water unbeknownst. I was so fucked up even after waking that I briefly considered leaving the hole unpatched, figuring it was better to see the pipes than not to.

"I relate to him. He hardly ever leaves the house now. He doesn't have friends anymore. He tries to make money, but sabotages himself. I think he's afraid of succeeding."

I take in what I've just said. I stare at the air-conditioning vent.

"Aaron is just like his brother," I say. "He can pick up any instrument and play it within five minutes. He has perfect pitch. We sing together sometimes, folk songs."

"How lovely."

"It's part of how we fell in love, harmonizing. I can only sing melody. Aaron harmonizes. We complement each other. He makes up for my deficits. We're very compatible. But also I think we're actually only compatible because he doesn't really know me."

"Oh?"

"He knows certain things about me, but they're surface-level things. He doesn't really know my baggage. I don't want to get into it. I like that he's still able to think that my limitations make me cute. Like, melody is the only part of the music I can hear. I can listen to any melody and sing it back to you perfectly, every note. Would you like me to sing for you?"

"Of course," he says.

"I suddenly don't want to."

"I am interested in anything you want to share with me."

"Then I'll sing for you," I say, "but not today."

"Not today," he says. "Perhaps when we're more comfortable together."

BEFORE EACH SESSION begins, I hand him a check for thirty-five dollars. This is the copay from my college insurance. The analyst tells me that this weekly payment is foundational to our partnership as analyst and analysand. If I forget the ceremony of paying him, he asks me why. I look within myself for a motive. I explain, "I know you deserve more than this." I want him to want to continue seeing me. After a month, I can't bear the thought of losing him. I feel as if I've invested too much in our relationship. I talk about him with all of my coworkers like he's my boyfriend. "My analyst tells me to 'have a decent afternoon,'" I tell them, smirking.

"Thank you for being patient with me," I say.

"You're most welcome," he says.

I lie on his couch with my shoes off. After standing for twelve hours, my feet ache. I went to a drawing class after my bookstore shift today and posed, then came here, and it will be another hour back to Kensington. I won't get home till nine o'clock.

"Aaron is suspicious of my every move," I say. "He needs to know where I'm going, who I'm out with, when I'll be home, every night. If I'm twenty minutes late, he starts calling me. He came around the corner of our apartment building the other day when I was finishing a phone call with a friend and demanded to know who I was talking to."

I say this like his paranoia's unthinkable. I was talking to a man I'd met on Instagram. I've become infatuated with his BDSM drawings and bought one for a hundred dollars just to begin a conversation with him. The drawing depicts a woman in a ball gag and handcuffs, with makeup running from her eyes. I hung it above my TV tray in the utility closet, telling Aaron, "I like this guy's work." I'd been messaging with him for two days when I got drunk with my coworker and asked him for his phone number, and called him on my way home. I'd just finished throwing up against the body of a train. I told him what happened and let him know I'd been masturbating thinking of him while my husband slept next to me. I was cackling. He messaged me later that night to say that I scared him. I asked him if he liked being afraid of me.

"He's especially suspicious of our friend Daniel," I say, "even though Daniel is having twins with my college roommate."

I haven't told the analyst about Heidi. I came across this information on Instagram on the same day I bought Tyler's drawing. I liked Heidi's announcement and commented, *Congratulations!*; then Daniel messaged me asking if we'd come to dinner. "He asked if we had any dietary restrictions," I told Aaron, laughing. "Doesn't he know you?"

"Daniel and I slept together once," I tell the analyst, "like five years ago. Aaron thinks I still want to fuck him."

"Do you?"

"Yes. But he's not special that way. I want to fuck a lot of people."

"How is he special?"

I close my eyes. We'd sat in their living room after dinner. Aaron and I drank wine; Heidi couldn't, with the fetuses; Daniel couldn't, as he was allegedly sober. I vaguely wondered about seeing him at the bar. My thigh pressed against his on the sofa. I leaned into him subtly, smelling the warmth of his neck. He hugged us at the door, and his hands rested in the small of my back. They were stable, familiar.

"I trust him," I say, opening my eyes. "And I don't trust Aaron. I don't want to have sex with Aaron anymore."

"Keep talking."

"I'm afraid of him. We argue, and for the rest of the day I can't even think of having sex with him. Then he guilts me into doing it or seduces me against my will. He touches me in a way he knows I've liked in the past and my body responds, I can't help it. I have sex with him, then I think I'm in love with him."

"Do you love him?"

"What do you mean?" I say. I think about it. "Of course I do." I reach for a tissue. "But I know this feeling of closeness is false—my body lying to me. He's using my body against me."

seventeen

I know you're never going to come visit me," my mother says to me on Thanksgiving. Aaron and I are spending the holiday at Aaron's parents' house, which I know she's salty about. She'll continue dropping her hurt feelings into otherwise pleasant conversations like chemical weapons for the foreseeable future. We invited her and my dad to join us, but my father was having dinner with his new girlfriend, and my mother was too self-righteous to fly up, though she claimed it was because she couldn't get the time off. "This is our busiest season." We're post-dessert, and I've stepped outside to call her from my in-laws' patio. It's freezing, as we're in the grip of a polar vortex. I welcome the excuse to distance myself, after performing interest in the turkey, the table settings, the music, and Aaron's brother's recent hobby of building computers in the attic.

"I don't have the money to fly, Mom," I say. "I'm sorry. Maybe you can help me."

"Save twenty dollars a week," she says.

"I don't have that. Aaron's out of work right now."

"You say you're struggling, but I've always struggled," she says, making my life about her, as always. "I've always had to be careful with money."

"I am careful with money."

"But I've always been diligent about putting money away," she says. "I'm sure you don't have to write at the coffee shop. Or you could bring your own coffee to the coffee shop. Or write at home."

"I can't write when Aaron's there. He doesn't leave me alone."

"You always date such clingy people."

"What do you mean by that?"

"You just always choose people who need you more than you need them. It's something I've noticed about you."

IN MY NEXT conversation with my mother, she spends the entire hour complaining about her own mother, because her recent decision to be outspoken about Uncle Bruce has driven the wedge between them even deeper. Nana is currently shrinking into her mattress in a new nursing home. I vent my frustration and exhaustion to the analyst, and then, feeling very fresh, sit down to share my hard-won analytical insights with my mother. I start by detailing all of the ways she's harmed me. Then I write, *It's because I love you that I hope you finally begin to heal from a lifetime of hurting. You have been through hell, and you have not done the necessary work to heal yourself. As a result, you pass your suffering on to others. Healing involves seeking therapy. With a therapist, examine why it is that you have always been so angry—I know there are many reasons. Examine why you consistently aim this anger at the people closest to you. Ask yourself why you continue to alienate people, and how it's affected your relationships, and how you can begin to repair them.*

I want to thank you for being so honest with me, she texts me minutes later. There is no way she could have absorbed my email in that time; I spent hours writing it. **There's no reason for me to explain or defend myself,** she says—in the first line, I'd accused her of being defensive whenever I raised an issue about our relationship. **You're completely**

right about how you feel, first of all because it's your personal truth, but mostly because it's reality. Then she says, Unfortunately, I don't have time or money for therapy.

Then I don't have time for this conversation, I say.

You've been in therapy for two months and you think you've figured everyone out.

I've been in therapy since high school.

So you have an honorary counseling license.

Therapy gives you tools.

I have tools.

She reminds me that she recently read a spiritual self-help book called *The Untethered Soul.*

MY MOTHER DOESN'T answer the phone for the next two months. She sends me to voicemail, then texts me and says, I'm working. She's been sick since Thanksgiving with a sinus infection that shows up as an enormous black hole in the X-ray of her face—she finally breaks the silence when she texts me a picture of it from the doctor's office. She refuses to take time off because she uses work to punish herself and barricade herself against her own life. "I fill in for everyone during holiday season," she says; then, "It's slow season and I'm making half of what I usually do, so I have to work twice as much." She loves being a martyr.

WHEN I ASK her, Are you mad at me? she says, No, sorry you think that.

We've barely talked in two months, I say.

I'm moving out of my apartment, she says. I've basically been living at Dara's.

Let me know if you want to talk about it, I say.

I don't have the time or energy right now.

I hope the new antibiotics are working.

I've been sick for a year but it's been nonstop since Thanksgiving.

What if I came April 17-19? I can ask for a day off.

It's honestly hard for me to take off work or have visitors that month, she says.

Can we talk about this on the phone?

You always call when I'm sleeping or at work and I can't answer. I'm sorry, I can't commit to anything with you right now.

I call Uncle Jude. After weeks of him ignoring my mother, she relented and saw his counselor with him. I believe he was hoping that, in that one magical meeting, she would awaken to the benefits of professional help and seek her own, but she hasn't.

"I'm worried about my mom," I tell him. "She's been sick for a long time and she won't answer the phone. I think she's mad at me, but I don't know why, and she says she's not, but I know she is. Did she say anything about me when you visited her?"

"I hardly saw her," he said. "She was working the whole time I was there. She arranged for me to go out to dinner with her and Dara one night, then she canceled at the last minute, so Dara and I went out together."

"Was she sick?"

"I don't know. She said she was tired."

I ASK MY mother for her address. She warns me that she rarely gets packages. People in her neighborhood steal them.

I mail her a gift of a bundle of palo santo. I include an abalone-shell stand and a handwritten card. *Hope this brings you some peace. Love you.*

Did you get my present? I text her a week later.

She responds the next day.

Yes, I told you I did.

AARON AGREES TO come with me to analysis. He also agrees to see the analyst alone, though he doesn't think he needs to. I intuit that he believes the problem with our relationship is me. His relenting to occasional therapy is a long con to show me how willing he is to change, though he has no intention of changing, and would have no idea how to go about doing so even if he did. No one in his family has ever been to therapy, and they have no vocabulary for talking about feelings, let alone taking responsibility for them—they are emotional idiots—"idiot" being another classic Firenze family insult. The Firenzes are loath to suffer idiots. To be an idiot is to renege on the individual's responsibility to know everything by knowing nothing. Knowing everything is the foundation of masculine identity, and the seat of power. A man should never be wrong, yet an idiot is wrong because he's "stupid." To be an idiot is emasculating. Women can also be idiots, but it's more common and less surprising when a woman is an idiot. It's almost like kicking a dog to call her one.

Aaron's intention is to turn this period of seeing the analyst around on me later: "I changed," he'll say, though he won't have. "It's your turn."

Aaron wants me to start "thinking of us as a unit." He thinks I think I'm better than he is, since he's a loser, though I've never said this aloud, and would never insult him to his face, except when I say things like, "What's wrong with you?" or, "What's your problem?"

"We're the same, Nina," he says. "We're equals."

"Yes, we agree on that," I say. What I don't say is "Then why don't you make more money?"

My hope is that my analyst will advocate for me. That, with therapeutic mind games, he will trick Aaron into becoming a less paranoid, more confident, more ambitious, less entitled individual who is solvent, listens, enjoys reading, and is happy entertaining himself now and again. Therapy scares Aaron—who knows what he'll find lurking in his own mind?—but I predict that once he meets my analyst, he will understand the allure, and quickly benefit from guided introspection. I can't afford more than one appointment for us per week, so Aaron and I now alternate week to week, and every third week, we go together.

"I've stopped thinking that our emotionally violent dynamic will change," I tell the analyst in our first couple's session. "I've been thinking of ways just to weather these storms better when they do blow in. I'm putting a lot of effort into it. I never know when something will set him off, and once an argument begins, there's no de-escalating it—he just loses all control. He followed me around the neighborhood for four hours last week, in the middle of the night. I just went for a walk to clear my mind."

"She told me she was going to throw herself in front of a bus."

"Excuse me, can I finish? Did you really think I would do that? No. I was exasperated. You'd been harassing me for hours." I turn to the analyst. "I was afraid to go home at that point. I was hiding behind trash cans."

We're in a different room than usual. This one has a sliding glass door to a meditation garden. The analyst looks bored. I ask him if he is. He says no.

"I'm afraid we'll never change," I say. "I can see why someone would tell me to leave, but then I doubt my own interpretation of events and think maybe I've imagined everything. And, of course, there's no such thing as absolute truth. Then I think, in many ways, we're perfect together, that no two people have ever been more perfect."

"She's trying to make me sound like some kind of abuser," says Aaron. "She slept with my best friend."

"Once, five years ago, before we were together."

"The problem is with the way we communicate," he says. "I know I'm guilty of it, too. We're more similar than I've heard her admit. I've been trying to break through to her, to show her that we do the same things to each other. It's just as hurtful when she does them to me. Do you know she cuts herself when we fight?"

The analyst listens.

"I know you know this. I know she talks to you about me. Her resistance to apologizing in the moment really bothers me. It upsets me when she storms away and slams the door. It just makes things worse."

"I'm not asking him to leave me alone forever," I say. "I'm asking for fifteen minutes."

"It would make me feel like she cared more if she could just apologize when I apologize, even if she doesn't completely mean it."

"He's not apologizing because he's sorry. He's apologizing so I'll shut up."

"Excuse me, can I finish?"

"I have legitimate reasons to be mad at him. After we fight, he acts like nothing is wrong. He jumps down my throat if he thinks I'm still upset."

"I just don't want us to be mad at each other."

"You don't get to tell me how to feel." I lean into it. "I'm not a robot. It's basic anatomy, Aaron. When you're angry, your brain floods with chemicals. My body thinks I'm being attacked."

"You're not," Aaron says. "You know that."

"Apparently I don't."

"It would just feel more balanced if you also apologized."

"Not this again."

"What? I'm allowed to have my own concerns. This is my session, too. There's an imbalance in our relationship. You're the one who dictates how we talk and when conversations begin and end."

"It's not ending when I ask you to give me space for fifteen minutes. We're putting it on hold. It means I can't hear you anymore. I'm too upset and I can't listen. At that point, you need to just leave me alone and let me calm down so I don't fly off the handle. You needle me and needle me until I explode. It's like you do it on purpose to piss me off and prove a point. I want to listen to you. I really do. I just can't in that moment. And I can't apologize. I'm too upset. You need to give me space. I'm fucking begging you, Aaron, for fifteen fucking minutes, to get the fuck out of my face."

He looks at the analyst. "See? Why is she swearing at me?"

I hate him. I want to harm him, and this is not who I am—I know I'm a peaceful person. I cried when I dropped a lizard in the air-conditioning unit when I was five. I didn't know what would happen, and the sound haunts me to this day. I learned something about time that day: I learned that a harm can never be undone. I'm not the kind of woman who hurts people. I know how it sounds, but I swear to God he makes me do it. He turns me into someone I'm not.

"She doesn't like the way I communicate? Me, either," he says, "but I'm trying really fucking hard to change it. Until then, this is just who I am and we're stuck with me communicating this way. She needs quiet time and space to think and do her writing. I sometimes have trouble giving it to her, but I've never asked her to stop needing it. I know she's not going to change that about herself. She doesn't think she has to."

"Are you hearing this shit?" I say.

The analyst listens.

"I'm tired of her not admitting the fact that how the two of us communicate is the problem," says Aaron. "That's what we need to work on. That's it."

I look at the analyst. "Please help me."

He sighs. He takes a long moment, choosing his words carefully. "There's a matter we must attend to before we address the way you communicate," he says. "You forgot to pay me."

AARON HATES THE analyst. He begins wearing sunglasses in our sessions. "These are prescription," he says when the analyst asks about them. He claims to have forgotten his other glasses. He thinks the analyst disapproves of his life choices and prefers me, though I've tried to explain to him that the ideal analyst is objective. The analyst would never admit it to me, since Aaron is now also his patient, and since, in general, the analyst says very little, and says nothing directly, and speaks only in riddles, but I believe he does think Aaron is a coward. In each of our couple's sessions, he asks him, "Mr. Firenze, why don't you want to make more money?" In our individual sessions, he asks me, "Why is Mr. Firenze trying to make you leave him?" I believe his intention is to remind Aaron and me that we have control over our choices. I choose to rescue, cling to, and lie to Aaron, while he chooses to use me and then silence me with incessant adoration.

I remind Aaron of his individual sessions with the analyst the day before each one, since he doesn't keep a calendar. "I don't do enough to necessitate using one," he's explained to me. I believe he would find it oppressive. After a few weeks of regular analysis, Aaron has satisfied himself that he's proven his willingness to change, and says, on the morning before his session, "I think I'm coming down with something."

The following week, he says, "I made plans tonight."

I often text the analyst, I will be coming instead of Aaron this evening.

Sometimes: Aaron will be coming with me this evening.

On a rare occasion, Aaron is coming instead of me tonight.

The analyst reminds me that classical analysis would have us all meeting every day. I feel that I'm failing us in the sense that the analyst has told me that he is also meant to benefit from our analytical partnership. In essence, I am also my analyst's analyst, and ideally we would, all of us, eventually, be able to "say everything."

I text the analyst between my now triweekly sessions to fill the gaps in communication. Aaron stays up all night, I say. I ask him when he's coming to bed and he screams at me. I was supine last night, hiding beneath the covers, and he was standing over me, screaming. My heart was pounding. I was afraid.

I want him to tell me it's time to leave Aaron. That this situation is growing dangerous, that I would be justified in escaping. He never says this.

I thank you for sharing these feelings, he responds, a few hours later. Will you be able to be safe enough until we talk about this on Thursday?

I construct the most professional response I can muster. I want to prove I'm not insane, that I didn't bring this upon myself. Even so, I long for him to see through me, to see how broken and scared I am, to come to me, take me by the arm, and lead me to a better life. Thank you, I say. Everything seems fine now. A read receipt appears, but he doesn't respond. I wait an hour, then follow up with him. It's as if nothing happened, I say. I'll be fine. I appreciate you listening.

Three dots appear. Disappear. Appear again.

Thank you for sharing your feelings and thoughts with me, he says.

On Thursday, I tell him, "He says he's 'useless,' 'stupid,' an 'idiot'—he uses these words because he knows I can't agree with him. He wants me to reassure him. But I can't force him to believe he's not a failure. And what evidence do I have? Do you hear my exhaustion?"

We're again in a different room. I've learned we keep moving because my analyst is a doctoral student at the center and the rooms are shared. This room is more air-conditioned. I stare at the vent, directly in the middle of my field of vision. I imagine climbing inside it, crawling on my hands and knees into the darkness. Below it someone has hung a framed print of John William Waterhouse's *Lady of Shalott*. My mother hung the same print in our Mylanta-blue bathroom when I was a child.

"I can't leave him," I say. "Divorce is expensive. I can't afford a lawyer. I'd have to find a new place to live. I can't afford to move. I can't afford to live alone. I don't know where I'd stay in the meantime. Certainly not with Aaron. Or my father. Or Leonard. Or any of my other coworkers. All of my friends hate me."

The Lady is lifting the chain of her boat, releasing herself downriver. Her expression is horror or rapture. A fall storm blows in; the world is thick with flowers. It's tragic the way she kills herself for the possibility of one true experience. A moment of ecstasy.

She saw for once in the mirror the flame-red helmet, the glinting armor, the shining saddle of Lancelot. She knows as she takes three strides toward the window that she will die for this, but she doesn't care. She beholds the world with her naked eye. The mirror shatters.

"I love Aaron," I say. This sounds wrong to me. "I love him," I say again, and I feel embarrassed. The analyst is quiet. "Are you awake?"

"Yes."

"He loves me and I worry what'll happen to him if I leave him. Where will he go? He'll think I've betrayed him."

"Ms. Wicks, can you experiment with the idea that you might want something?"

The Lady's tapestry tells the world of her curse. The only way they'll ever know her. She's dead by the time she reaches Camelot. The townspeople gather around her. They find a parchment on her chest, her final statement, but it is not addressed to Lancelot. He's nowhere in sight. She didn't expect him to be. She fled for her fantasy, to die with it.

"I want to be alone," I tell him. "I want everyone to leave me the fuck alone. My monogamous relationships all overlap. I don't know how it happens. I'm not looking for it. I feel like my life is mocking me. I watch myself doing things and I don't know why. I don't even recognize myself. I don't know who this is inside my body."

"Who do you think?"

eighteen

I graduate and lose my insurance. I thought it would last through the summer, but at Walgreens my NuvaRing costs a hundred dollars and I have fifty-six dollars in my bank account, so I leave without buying it. It's Monday and payday is Thursday, and all we have in the kitchen is a can of kidney beans, old pancetta, browning basil, and a box of fusilli. We've stopped asking Aaron's parents to buy us groceries, to spare ourselves the humiliation. For dinner tonight, we'll eat whatever is left over at the bookstore café after it closes: a muffin and Italian wedding soup from a bladder maybe, or chocolate croissants and a bagel that aren't claimed by other booksellers—everyone has a side hustle, and everyone is broke.

To sign onto the store's insurance would take a hundred dollars out of each paycheck. My hormones spike the first day without the ring. By the third day, I'm raging.

"I never want to take birth control again," I tell the other Nina. She's straightening design books in the natural light of the store's entryway. I've learned she has poor boundaries for an employer. She may be my friend, or she may be my mentor, or she may be my rival—it changes day to day as different booksellers fall in and out of her favor. She's the Regina George of intelligent retail.

Perhaps her problem is that, like many wealthy people in New York, Nina feels guilty about her privilege. Or perhaps she suffers from malaise, longs for the vitality of the rabble, wants to be one of us, then blames and resents us for failing to absolve her of self-loathing. She emails me at one in the morning, *Why is the early-reader spinner out of order?* Then she takes me out for lunch at Balthazar and overshares—"When my sister gave birth, she split to the anus."

"I track my fertility," she says, facing out five copies of *Living with Pattern*.

"With an app?"

She walks to the Parenting section and scans the Pregnancy shelf. I feel a fire in my vaginal canal, and it's ever creeping northward, through my belly and nipples.

"I had no idea what it meant to have a libido," I say, sure she can smell me. "I've been on mute since high school."

She hands me a hefty tome with a CD-ROM glued to the inside.

"*Taking Charge of Your Fertility*," I say, turning it over. Deep fuchsia petals decorate the softcover. "And this actually works?"

She shrugs. "So far."

I BRING IT home to show Aaron. The pages are illustrated with full-color close-up photographs of white women's fingers testing the viscosity of their cervical fluid.

"Is this sticky?" I ask him, holding up some of my own.

The first thing we learn is that the book teaches the Fertility Awareness Method, which is not the same as the rhythm method. The Fertility Awareness Method is based on the concept of empowerment through education. Here is a contraceptive that works 99.4 percent of the time without hormones or implantations, it says, but instead through diligence and communication between partners. Each morning, I reach for a clipboard and a basal thermometer and, after peeing, check my cervical position with two fingers shoved inside, swirling around in a circle. If my cervix is low and soft, if I'm full and slick, there's no question I'm fertile.

I'm attaching the exercise we discussed about how to handle the fertile phase, says my new fertility counselor, Ilaria. I reached out to her looking for guidance after a month, unable to ignore the fact that Aaron was not as invested in Fertility Awareness as I was. After I explained our financial situation, Ilaria agreed to a free Skype consultation. The tone in her follow-up email is troubled. *For now, I advise that you use some kind of barrier method whenever you have intercourse, except for the first 5 days of the cycle.* During my fertile week, we're supposed to choose abstinence, but my hormonal surge means we have to exercise a special willpower. We try to use condoms or spermicide, but we hate condoms and spermicide. *When you're "highly fertile," I recommend you either stick to oral, or use a combination of methods, like condom + withdrawal. Condoms sometimes fail.*

THERE HASN'T BEEN blood in my underwear in six weeks. There's only a clear vaginal discharge and my swollen labia. My cervix is low and hard. My breasts are tender. I take a pregnancy test on my lunch break, and for the rest of my shift, I stand behind the register Googling images of babies in different stages of development. According to my fertility calendar, my embryo is the size of a poppy seed. It has eye pigment, lungs, a heart, and a single layer of translucent skin. No arms or legs. A mutant seahorse.

I feel no sense of protectiveness over it. Instead I feel it's invaded my personal space. In another week, its heart will begin beating and it will be as big as a peppercorn and have blood vessels, a spinal cord, and a brain. My abdomen will be full and thick; my nipples will chafe; I'll cry on the subway, sleep in the break room with ginger tea, have no desire to be touched. Other people will smell toxic to me. A week later, it will have bones and muscles. I gaze at the tip of my finger and imagine a poppy seed on it. I feel as if every eye in the store is on me. I decide to swear off coffee and alcohol; my body no longer belongs to me. I'm starving but queasy, overwhelmed. I long for a cigarette.

On the train, I give my seat up for a pregnant woman. I want her to see me, hold me. I rest my palm on my abdomen to communicate to her that I'm in pain. I imagine the parasite needing me. I find that I love it in a certain way for this. I decide to eat dairy, legumes, sweet potatoes, and salmon. I'm a nurturing person.

I call my father to ask him for the money. We haven't talked since his new girlfriend answered his phone and I was forced to converse with her for several minutes while he finished in the bathroom. I'm glad he's able to hold down a relationship, but she had a Floribama accent that made me want to kick through the wall. He tells me that I'm the age my mother was when she had me, and reminds me that I'm married, and I think he must be saying this to hurt me. I sit on the edge of my bathtub gazing at our grooming appliances.

"It's five hundred dollars," I say, using Aaron's nail clippers to excise a layer of dead skin from my thumb. "I'll never ask you for anything ever again. I make fourteen dollars an hour, Dad. Please." I know I'm privileged and selfish.

AARON COMES WITH me to the clinic. My fetus is the size of a raspberry as I sit two chairs away from him in the waiting room. The news is on, and the air is uncomfortably warm and smells of takeout. Trump is yakking about his border wall. Last month he was hawking taco bowls in Trump Tower. I could vomit. There's been a shooting in Orlando and forty-nine people are dead. I text my mother. **Everyone okay?** That anyone would have children astounds me, since it feels like there won't be a world left in thirty years. I read somewhere that having biological children is the second worst thing you can do for global warming, after flying in an airplane.

A pregnant woman beside me struggles to her feet, reaches for the remote, and hits the power button. The room falls silent. For the last three weeks, while waiting for my abortion, I've secluded myself, avoiding the news, too sensitive for this planet, avoiding human contact. I don't want comfort. I don't want to share this private transformation I'm undergoing in which I'll become monstrous.

I burrow into my grief. I'm morbidly curious about viable pregnancies. I angle away from Aaron and navigate to Heidi's Instagram, where lately I can tell she's taking steps to broaden her audience, and springboard her pregnancy into a brand. She's tagged the manufacturer of some raw-cotton onesies she's styled in a draping formation over her naked baby bump. Each minute I spend pondering this, my fetus grows one hundred new brain cells. I put my phone in my purse on airplane mode. I rub my face and press my middle fingers into my eyeballs. Aaron comes over to me. "What's wrong?" he asks, as if it's not obvious. His show of contrition irritates me. A baby would bind us indelibly, which he may have wanted, and I delight in a small measure seeing him suffer. If only our "circumstances," as he calls them, had been different, we could have had a baby, he says, so thank fuck we're destitute.

Women recline in the back hallway, beneath fleece. We avoid eye contact. I ask the nurse whether fetuses can feel what's happening to them. "If you're not sure, don't do it," she responds.

We take the prescription she gives me to the Walgreens across the street, then eat at a sidewalk café. I swallow the first two pills with ice water. I feel relief as I imagine them halting the growth in my womb. We are children, but we could have been more childish; we made an adult decision. Aaron says, "We'll have kids when we're ready." I smile.

I carry my dead fetus through the following workday and let the rest of the pills dissolve in my cheeks when I get home. What follows is agonizing. Aaron holds me in the bathtub. Blood disappears in the water like light diffusing. The burning comes in waves. I wake in the darkness hours later with a heating pad tied around my waist. I am sodden with my own blood.

IN THE BATHROOM across the hall from the analyst's office, I pass a clump of tissue the size of my thumb. It comes out as I'm wiping. I hold it in my palm and feel its weight. It's dense and gray, like the dirt of Odessa's grandma's yard when we were kids. I call up a memory of walking with Odessa to the city park from her grandma's house one day. By the lake we found a mother duck on a nest of eggs. We fought her off with a stick to steal two of them. We tried to hatch them in her bedroom, carried them in our underwear and experimented with different ways of keeping them warm: our armpits, wrapped in blankets, hidden under her pillows. Then we grew impatient. We took them outside as it was starting to rain. We counted to three before swinging dumbly at the trunk of a palm tree. The eggs broke in our hands. There were baby ducks inside them, fully formed, sleeping, slick with goo and blood; then the screen door opened and Odessa's grandma scolded us back into the house. We watched through the windows as she buried them.

I consider wrapping the clump in a cloth. I could take it home and hide it somewhere, perhaps in a wooden box on the shelf above our bed. It would decompose and smell. Aaron would discover it and make me throw it away. I remember hearing a story about a girl who was arrested in the Herald Square Victoria's Secret when security noticed a smell emanating from her large handbag. They found her dead newborn inside it, wrapped in plastic bags stashed below stolen bras and underwear. She'd delivered him the day before in her friend's bathtub. Her friend was at Victoria's Secret with her. "You don't understand life until you have a child," the mother told a *Vice* reporter. "You don't understand love." She was seventeen and had two other children. One couldn't be located. One visited her on Rikers Island on the weekends.

I fold the clump in a tissue. I close it in my hand and hold it up to my lips and breathe in the smell, warm and smoky, sweet with a yeasty afternote. I stand from the toilet, drop it into the bowl, and flush.

"I dreamt I was visiting the Grand Canyon with Aaron's family," I tell the analyst. This is our last session. I can't afford him anymore. Without insurance his base rate is $250, nonnegotiable. "We were standing in two lines approaching the precipice," I say. "One red line and one blue line. You had to choose a line but I didn't know what for. I had the feeling that I was missing something. I knew I wouldn't get to see what I'd gone there to see."

"What did you go to see?" he asks me.

"We reached the front and Aaron's mother was standing there. She was granting people passage and she held a long staff. At the top of the staff was a fishbowl with a baby inside it," I say. "And ribbons streaming down."

"What color were they?"

"White," I say. "Yellow."

I email him later. *We want you to know how grateful we are for all that you've taught us,* I say. I don't want to leave him. I want him to help me process my grief. I want him to read through these lines, to see the searing, silent begging beneath them. *You've helped us immeasurably, both together and independently. Our lives and our partnership have only benefited from our relationship with you. We know you've made allowances for our financial and temporal limitations, and we want you to know your generosity has not gone unnoticed or unappreciated. We hope that, when our schedules settle, and our finances permit, we can find a way to reinitiate our sessions with you. Until then, we wish you health, happiness, and success. With all our love and gratitude, Nina & Aaron.* He doesn't respond.

A week later, I Google him. I find his Facebook, but it's private. I find his LinkedIn, but it's sanitized. I wrap his name in quotes and find an article he wrote for an ultraconservative libertarian website.

The title is "Diagnosed with Liberalism." He's taken as the basis for his authority his experience as a psychoanalyst.

The loss of the American family unit is the single most destructive force to befall us in the modern era. When the father is not present in the home to set the structure of the family unit, a sense of anxiety takes hold and leads to externally directed hostility. Soon the patient is looking to the outside world to show her what her limits are. She acts out in hopes society will control her. Her desire for paternal law becomes pathologized.

PC violations, their narcissistic injury, their petulance—which is itself fear-driven—become dangerous when one's ideology comprises one's identity. It's as though, when that happens, rationality and socialization dissolve. The ideologically identified patient can often become wildly reckless. She seeks the obscuring of accountability by means of increased pathos.

"POLITICAL CORRECTNESS IS killing us," says Aaron's father. I observe Aaron's brother disassociate. He bends down over his lasagna, shrinking into himself until he can once again escape into the attic to hand-solder equipment for Aaron's eventual movie set. "The fact is, the shooter was a radical Islamist," says his father.

"That's not what he said, actually," I say. "He said 'Islamic terrorist' and called Islam a 'hateful foreign ideology.'"

"What's the difference?"

"And therein lies the problem."

"See? How can I have a conversation with people like you?"

"Like me?"

"I'm a registered Democrat, but far-left liberals today are another species."

"The point is that Trump is a racist."

"I agree with you, but the left today is a circular firing squad."

"Okay, I've had enough of this conversation," says Aaron's mother, reaching for more bread. Aaron promised he wouldn't tell his parents about my abortion, but his mother hasn't looked at me since we arrived.

"Is there a problem?" I say.

She butters her bread.

"Cathy?"

"I'm not feeling well," she says.

"Oh no," says Aaron. "Are you sick?" He leans over and places his hand on her shoulder, then smooths her hair. He lays his other hand on her forehead. "Mom?"

"I'm fine," she says, setting down her bread and knife. She places her hand on her stomach. "Just a little nauseous."

"Let me get you a Tums."

He escapes down the hallway.

"My mother's girlfriend lost a friend in the shooting," I say.

"I'm sorry to hear that," says his father.

"My dad's company is pitching Trump's campaign," says Aaron's brother, suddenly laughing.

"It's not my company," says Aaron's father. "I'm a consultant, and it's a one-year contract to help a video startup pitch advertising."

"But you're pitching the Trump campaign?" I say.

"It's business," he says. "We're also pitching Bernie."

nineteen

I go to the corner dive bar to enlist the aid of the outside world in my self-abuse. Aaron is at his parents' house for the next three days while his mother recovers from gallbladder surgery. I should be with him, but I pretended to be unable to cover my shifts at the bookstore. The bar's backyard is decorated with string lights, and I'm drinking a neat, peaty Scotch and lighting a cigarette when I see Daniel sitting by himself at one of the picnic tables. At first I'm disappointed. I'd wanted to be alone, just not isolated, to gaze at those in my midst as though through a milky scrim. Daniel is discreetly watching the family at the next table. Their baby sleeps in a sling. I see no way around saying hi.

"Cute baby," I say. "Where's Heidi?"

"At her mom's for a few days."

His chin is covered in stubble. His eyes are glassy.

"So is Aaron," I say. "His mom had gallbladder surgery."

"Sounds serious."

"The surgeon estimated four hundred gallstones. It was completely septic."

"Gross."

He turns his can of beer in a circle, looking at it.

"How have you been?" I say.

"Can you keep this between us?"

I nod.

"We lost one of the twins."

I recognize his decision to sit near the baby as self-destructive. She's oblivious to the ways time is already closing off possibilities, how her ever-expanding experience will be inversely limited by perspective, biology, anatomy, circumstance, other people. She will never be the best at what she does. She will suffer.

"It's not uncommon," he says. "It happens in one in three multiple pregnancies."

"Do you find that comforting?"

He shrugs.

"I had an abortion two weeks ago and I'm still bleeding," I say.

"Is that normal?"

"I'm trying to think of it as a loving act. My parents should never have had me."

"I went through it with my ex. It was difficult."

We sit in silence. I finish my Scotch and offer Daniel a cigarette. Beside us the baby shits and her dad takes her to the bathroom. I feel badly for Daniel, watching her leave. I want to do him a favor. I decide to let him take care of me.

"Do you have a Xanax?"

"I'M NOT USED to being alone." We're sitting on the fire escape of his building, curled against the brick in our socks. "But inside I'm kind of a lone wolf." I pass the blunt back to him. The night is cool and fresh. We're three floors above the street. Below us the bodega light is blinking. "I haven't had this feeling of isolation since I first got out of rehab. It's not a feeling I've ever been able to cope with. I got into a really stupid relationship right away just to escape it. Maybe that makes me codependent."

"Maybe everyone's codependent," he says.

"When I was a teenager, I'd come home to an empty house and eat cheese quesadillas from the microwave because I didn't know how to cook anything. Nobody taught me. Even before my mother left, she never cooked. We ate TV dinners. That's what that feeling reminds me of. By high school, I wouldn't see my dad until ten o'clock, and then he would just watch TV until he went to bed. He wouldn't even notice that I was drunk. I would be sitting next to him on the couch, but we never interacted, he never got close enough to smell me."

He passes me the blunt.

"Would you say you're a lonely person?" I say.

"I lost most of my friends when I started touring. I was fucked up a lot of the time. I got a whole new set of friends, but then I alienated them acting like an asshole. A lot of people won't work with me, not that I care. I'm still trying to figure out what I want to do with my music, if I even want to make music anymore. I'm kind of sick of it."

"That's how I felt when I left school. Nobody even tried to find me. Only Aaron."

"I'm sorry I didn't reach out."

"I didn't expect you to."

We look at each other. I move my hand to his elbow and cradle it. I hit the blunt, and he reaches for it, but I hold it away from him.

"Shotgun," I say.

I lean into him. I place my mouth lightly over his. He hesitates, but I exhale. Smoke falls from his mouth.

THE SUN IS a bright ball. I reach for my phone on Daniel's nightstand and find eleven missed calls from Aaron. *Hey, sweetie,* he says from my voicemail, *I guess you're still sleeping, but my mom is feeling pretty good, actually, so I'm coming home this morning, and she's just gonna call me if she needs anything. I'm excited to see you, I missed you last night. Leaving here soon. Okay, I love you.*

Hey, cutest, it's nine o'clock, wow, this is late for you, but I'm glad you're sleeping 'cause I bet you were up late writing. I know you have a hard time sleeping when you're alone. Okay, I'm coming over the bridge, so I should be seeing you in, like, half an hour if the traffic's not too bad. I love you so much, you're perfect and beautiful, okay, bye.

Hey, um, I just got back to our apartment. You're not here. I'm a little worried. Did I forget that you're working this morning? I thought you were on the schedule for this afternoon? Are you at the supermarket or something? Please call me.

Nina, where are you? I've been sitting here for an hour and I called the bookstore and they told me you're not even on the schedule today. I'm extremely worried. I hope nothing has happened to you. I'm ready to call the police. Please call me.

There are no more voicemails, just unanswered calls and an onslaught of texts that grow increasingly irate. It's eleven thirty. My blood is glacial as I think of any possible way to not go home. I consider calling Daniel to my defense. He could tell Aaron that I called him because I was distraught, that I was having a panic attack and had to sleep on his couch.

I shake Daniel.

"Hey," I say. "I have to go. Can we please keep this between us?" He looks anemic. "Please just keep this between us, okay?"

I call Aaron on the sidewalk. "Sweetie, I'm so sorry. I didn't realize you were calling me. I had my phone in my backpack. I walked all the way to the Brooklyn Bridge just now. I've been walking for three hours." My heart is racing. "Aaron? I didn't stop to look at my phone, sweetie, I'm so sorry you were worried."

"You didn't stop to look at your phone even one time in three hours?" he says.

"No, I didn't."

"You didn't stop to use the bathroom somewhere, or stop to buy anything and take your phone out of your backpack out of habit?"

"Aaron, no. I really didn't. I'm so sorry." I begin speed-walking toward our apartment. The sidewalk is a crush of children and dogs. "Are you there?"

"It just seems unlike you to walk all the way to the Brooklyn Bridge for no reason."

"You're out of town," I say. "I couldn't sleep at all. I was wide-awake at six o'clock and I don't want to sit around the house by myself."

"You said you were working today."

"I'm sorry. I just needed alone time."

"My mother had surgery."

"I know. I'm sorry."

He's silent. I begin running.

"You just got up first thing in the morning and had nothing else to do, and felt inspired to go on a three-hour walk?"

"Aaron, yes."

I listen to dead air, a sound like wind rushing past.

"Where are you?" he says.

"Are you in the car right now?"

"Yeah, I can come pick you up. Where are you?"

"I'm ten minutes away. I just got to the bottom of Prospect Park. There's a horse-drawn carriage here. We should ride one sometime. I've always wanted to do that."

There's a long silence.

"Just tell me what street you're on."

"I don't see a street sign, Aaron. Hang on."

I sprint for several seconds. When I can't anymore, I stop and look at the map on my iPhone and pick a spot several blocks away that I think I can get to by the time he reaches it.

I SIT AGAINST a stone wall, panting and sweating, and watch a colony of ants descend on a dying monarch writhing at my feet. They approach it, climb onto it, then retreat to tell their friends about its weakness. They return with an army to eat it alive. The butterfly is too sick to fight them. It moves its legs, tries to walk away, tries to fly, stumbles and falls. I lift it by a wing and blow the ants away. I spit on the ground to give them food and my viscous saliva lands on a clump, drowning them. I crush the trapped ones with my toe to put them out of their misery. Their friends come to eat them. I watch the monarch open and close its wings in my palm, blameless.

Aaron pulls up with his window open. "Hey," I say. "Look what I found." I climb into the passenger seat and cup the butterfly against the wind, demonstrating how gentle I can be. "I'll euthanize it in the freezer when we get home."

He pulls away from the curb.

"I'M NOT LYING," I say.

Aaron's sitting on top of his desk. Leaning against it is his red secondhand Telecaster, on which he's currently teaching himself to play the following selections from *Blood Sugar Sex Magik*: "The Power of Equality," "If You Have to Ask," "Breaking the Girl," "I Could Have Lied," "The Righteous and the Wicked," "Give It Away," "Naked in the Rain," and "Sir Psycho Sexy."

"What streets did you take?" he says.

"I went through the park to Grand Army Plaza and Fort Greene to the Brooklyn waterfront."

"And you didn't take any pictures of the waterfront?"

"I was enjoying not looking at my phone."

"Then why bring it?"

"In case of an emergency."

He turns back to the window. It's open only a sliver at the bottom, though the room is a hundred degrees. His cigarette nauseates me, but if I ask him to put it out or open the window further, I'll seem passive-aggressive. We've tried to brighten the desk with lilies he bought me with my debit card, which I had given him to buy cigarettes, since he's unable to buy his own, since he owes Wells Fargo a hundred dollars and refuses to pay it back on principle because "Wells Fargo has stolen billions of dollars from the American people."

"Then why did you have me pick you up at Stratford and Church? It doesn't make sense that you would be over there if you went through the park."

"I must have gotten lost."

He walks to the kitchen and very calmly pours himself a glass of water. The air in the room feels as if it will detonate. He walks back to the desk and chugs the entire glass looking out the window. I watch him. He sets the glass down again.

"I know you were with Daniel," he says, observing the street. "Please tell me the truth."

"I wasn't."

"I know you were. I talked to Heidi. She's in Boston and Daniel isn't with her."

"Well, I didn't know that," I say. I wonder whether Heidi is having a similar conversation right now with Daniel. "Why were you talking to Heidi?"

"I think you know."

"I really don't."

"I'm calling Daniel."

"Go ahead."

The window shatters. Tiny pieces of glass land on his shoulders and in his hair. The base of the window has broken into jagged angles. A stream of blood drags from Aaron's forehead to his nose, down to his chin. I breathe into my hands. I'm shaking.

He bangs his bloody head against the wall.

"Stop it," I say. I place my hand on his forehead. My fingers are warm with blood. I lead him to the bathroom and sit him on the lid of the closed toilet. I look into his face.

"There are no carriages in Prospect Park," he says.

"What?"

"You think I'm a piece of shit, so you fucked Daniel."

I grab a conditioner bottle and throw it as hard as I can against the wall. It breaks open, sliding in iridescent lines down the plaster. I want to destroy him. I want to light his corpse on fire. "I didn't fuck Daniel," I say.

"Why would you lie to me?"

"Because I hate you."

"You shouldn't say things you don't mean."

I shove him.

"This is abusive," he says.

"Shut the fuck up," I say. "Shut the fuck up, you piece of shit."

I wrench open the shower. I shove him forward into the water and shampoo the glass from his hair. He bleeds on the towels as I dry him. I press a corner of one onto the gash and tell him to hold it there while I find the Krazy Glue. When I return, he's taken the towel away from his forehead and is purposely bleeding all over himself. I pinch the two sides of the broken skin together.

"You need to hold still," I say.

He pulls away, and I grab a fistful of his hair. I look him in the eye as I use my thumbs to close the wound. I wipe the excess glue away with the towel, and filaments of cotton lint remain behind. Aaron gives up fighting. His head falls back limply against my stomach.

"You scare me," I say.

twenty

I shut down all communication. I lock myself in the bathroom once a day and cut myself with a broken Bic razor. Aaron discovers this while I'm walking around naked one day, after a shower. I let him know in so many words that he's responsible. His clinginess and suspicion, and constant, low-grade criticism of me—compounding my burden as our home's primary breadwinner—have driven me to this extreme; it is my only outlet. I begin taking notes toward a memoir about leaving my husband, hoping I will force myself to finish it, but weeks go by and I can't seem to turn my rough outline into prose. I don't communicate with Daniel. I act like he doesn't exist. I continue to deny ever seeing him that night, and assume he corroborates my story because we don't hear from Heidi—it's as if we were never sort-of-friends with them. When we see their baby on Instagram, we don't discuss it.

We broke the lock on the bathroom door during one of our fights, so I announce aloud when I have to shit. Aaron comes in anyway to get something from the cabinet. A turd plops. "Oh, sorry," he says, with no urgency. He proceeds to retrieve the item. "Okay, okay," he says when I tell him to leave. A small animal has been moving through my colon since the morning after I slept with Daniel. I've learned from WebMD that I can in fact be constipated while having chronic diarrhea because the liquid flows around the obstructions.

The discomfort of constipation blends with the lingering tenderness of my pelvic floor muscles from the abortion. A hemorrhoid on my anus has healed with a flap of skin remaining behind like a flag. I tried to remove it by cutting off blood flow with dental floss, but this only served to cause an infection and has left behind an open sore.

Aaron still tries to rim me, which is painful and humiliating, but I can only bring myself to admit this sometimes, trying to spare the last of his manhood. I'm repelled by the thought of having any kind of sex with him, but if I turn him down two days in a row, he starts crying, and though I think of myself as someone who is comfortable with men crying, I've found this to only be true in theory. Aaron asks me for reports on my bowel movements, trying to be supportive and sympathetic. He wants to know when I'll be back to normal, ready to fuck him. He thinks I don't love him anymore. "How was it?" he asks every time I leave the bathroom.

ODESSA CALLS ME, and I happen to be headed to the subway, which provides a temporal limit to our conversation, so I answer and tell her she has ten minutes. I anticipate her telling me something along the lines of her being at the police station with Ian because he robbed a 7-Eleven and was caught with someone else's Suboxone. Trees are turning amber and littering the ground in crushed leaves. I pass a wall of vines with sparrows flitting into the thin cover they provide. "It's nice to hear your voice," I say.

"You won't believe where I am right now," she says. Her sniffle is meant to signal that she's crying. She pauses for effect. "I'm at the hospital. Mission died last night."

I stop walking.

"They managed to resuscitate him. They called me at six o'clock this morning to come get him."

I lean against a garden gate, check the time, and decide that I don't care if I'm late for work. I'll tell the bookstore someone died. I drop my backpack.

"He was squatting at a house in Roser Park, shooting heroin with crusties," she says. "He overdosed and they dumped him outside the ER."

"Is he still homeless?"

"He's been couch-surfing since you broke up with him."

"I thought he would've found a place by now."

"Of course you did."

"I thought you hated him."

"I saw him at Zine Fest and he gave me a Steel Reserve. We did key bumps in the alley."

"Did he say anything about me?"

"Does that matter right now?" I realize she's calling to blame me for Mission's overdose. He's given her the idea that I ruined his life—that if I'd stayed with him, none of this would have happened. I'm where his downfall began. "He's going to be okay," she says. "Not that you asked, but he should be fine."

"I'm so glad," I say.

I imagine him sleeping on a bare wood floor littered with cat shit. Flushing the toilet with a bucket of rainwater. Jamming a dirty needle into the back of his hand. He'd wanted me to drop off the grid with him, escape the ever-present eyes of the NSA, Illuminati, and New World Order, somewhere in the disused suburbs of Berlin. I threw him out to avoid that fate. Odessa thinks I should have stayed and guarded him from it.

"Why did he call you to pick him up?" I ask her. "Why didn't he call his mother or one of his crusty friends?"

She's quiet.

"'Dessa?"

"And so will I, Nina. I had a hard morning, I haven't eaten yet, but I'll be fine. Thanks for your concern."

"Don't be like that."

"My friend died today, and I'm here to be with him while my daughters hang out with the senile old lady next door, possibly drowning or choking, but don't worry about us. We're all good over here."

A hedge rustles. A piss-stenched hobo appears in my periphery, asking for change. I ignore him and he asks for my phone number. I tell him to fuck off and he threatens to shut me up with his dick.

"What was that?" says Odessa.

"Someone asking for change."

"Did you give him any?"

"No, I don't have any."

"Really, Nina?"

"Yes, Odessa. I'm poor, remember? My husband doesn't work, and my job pays minimum wage, and I don't carry cash because it costs money to use the ATM, and I can't even get approved for a credit card. Whenever I try, my credit score plunges. Is that what you want to hear? Am I struggling enough for you?"

"It just seems unlikely that you don't have any change."

"Why did you even call? To be a cunt? I'm sorry you're having a shitty day. Sorry you're cranky about it. I've already been through all that shit with Mission. There's a reason I broke up with him three fucking years ago. It's sad that he's not doing well. He wasn't doing well when I met him. I gave him a real life, which he didn't appreciate. You want to take care of him? Have fun being yet another person's mother."

I hang up.

The bum has snuck into the garden next door and is tugging his meat behind a shrub, watching me. I turn away, pick up my backpack, and continue walking toward the subway. I reach the intersection and an SUV cuts close to the corner, almost taking me out. Odessa calls me back. "You think I'm white trash," she says when I answer to say, "I'm not doing this."

"It's fine," she says. "I am."

"What does that even mean?"

"It means you think you're better than me. You're a big New Yorker now, a married lady, publishing one shitty book review in the *Brooklyn Rail*, and now you think I'm beneath you. Is this conversation even real, Nina, or is it all copy for you?"

"You're a very talented person, Odessa," I say. "You're so smart, so charismatic."

"I don't need you to reassure me."

"I just wonder what you could have done with your life if you hadn't had a baby right out of middle school."

"I wonder what you would have done if your nana hadn't paid for your fancy-ass grad school."

"Maybe you could have gone to college or pursued acting. Or biology? Politics? Travel? Become a high-class hooker? Moved to New York with Dennis as your sugar daddy? I just wonder what kind of life you could have made for yourself. It's too bad you can't go back in time."

"Yeah, I know what you mean," she says. "I just wonder if you ever feel something fundamental is missing inside you, Nina? Like there's a void inside you that can't be filled and probably never was? Part of being a decent person that you just don't have so all that's left of you is a really horrible bitch that no one can stand?"

"Maybe," I say.

I BEGIN GOING to poetry readings because I know Aaron won't want to come with me. He doesn't understand poetry and feels threatened by male poets and their ability to be femme and sexually irresistible even when they're ugly. He's threatened by what he terms their "poet coats," and their illegible references to Tikkun and Hegel and Simone Weil. These poets are more prone to talk about panda videos, Lana Del Rey, carnivorous plants, and David Lynch, but he doesn't need to know that. "Tube worms are fascinating," I say to a group smoking and shivering outside the Poetry Project on a Monday night. "But also narcissistic. They brag about not having anuses, but look closer: the bacteria inside them have anuses."

"We talking about Melania?" says one, joining the circle.

My phone rings and I see that it's Daniel. I consider not answering it since Heidi recently blocked me on Instagram, which I take as a bad sign. When I lurked on my finsta, I saw that all of her photos were of the baby; there were none of Daniel. It's ten o'clock, and outside the church it's freezing, the first plummet, but inside it's too quiet for conversation. He calls again, then texts me: I'm sorry to bother you, but I really need to talk to someone.

I walk a few yards toward the street.

"I don't know how to tell you this," he says. "I tried to kill myself. I took a drill bit to my wrist."

"What?" I say. I look back toward the group, which is beginning to file back inside for the reading. I walk around the courtyard of the church and crouch against a wall. "Where are you?"

"I'm fine. It was a month ago. I have limited mobility in my hand now," he says. "I can't play guitar. Frankly, I'm embarrassed more than anything." He breathes into the receiver.

"I'm so sorry," I say. "I didn't know."

"Listen, I need to ask you something."

"Sure, anything."

"You said you loved me that night. Did you mean it?"

"What night?"

"That night."

I search that night at his apartment, then realize he's talking about college.

"I was wondering if you'd meet me in person."

"I can't tonight, I'm sorry."

"Are we friends, Nina?"

"Of course we are."

"Do you still want to be my friend?" He's crying.

"Of course I'm your friend, Daniel. Of course I am."

We pick a bar in the East Village. It takes him thirty minutes to get there. When we hug, he gives off a thick, sweet smell, like old laundry. I examine the feeling that forms in my gut, sick with knowing something I can't pinpoint. He smiles with his teeth, a bit too happy. We take our drinks to a corner.

"It's good to see you," I say.

"I told you I wasn't done with you," he says.

I look at his hands. I see no scar in the space between his palm and his sleeve. The bottom of his sleeve is streaked gray.

"Where are you staying?" I ask.

"On the floor of my friend's art studio."

"How long have you been there?"

"A few weeks."

He looks up from the table, and his pupils are dilated. I watch him struggle to form words. "She has her own reasons which I dare not impart upon," he says, attempting a British accent. His hand rests on my hand. "Do you know why I asked you here?"

He leans in to kiss me and I turn away. He brings my chin toward him with his other hand.

"Daniel, please," I say.

I leave my body as he slides toward me around the booth. I watch myself from the next table. He kisses me and pushes his hand inside my waistband. His finger enters me halfway. My pussy burns from the lingering imbalance of the abortion.

"Listen, I'm here for you," I say, moving away, suddenly returning. I take his hands in mine. His finger is sticky. "Daniel, you know I'm your friend, right?"

He's crying. He places my hand on his dick through his jeans. I stroke him compassionately.

"Everything will be okay," I say. "I have to go home now."

He holds my face in his hands. I try to pull away from him, but he won't let me.

"Let go, Daniel," I say gently. He doesn't. I realize my hand is still on his dick and remove it. I pry his fingers from my hair. "You're hurting me," I say.

"I'm sorry," he says as I stand to leave.

"You have nothing to apologize for."

"I'm sorry, Nina."

"Talk to you later, Daniel."

I check my phone on the train. **I wrote this song for you,** he's texted. It's a Spotify link to U2's "With or Without You." I block him.

I DEVELOP A yeast infection from the mix of Daniel's dirty fingers and old blood. I try to cure it naturally with a clove of garlic wrapped in cheesecloth shoved up my vaginal canal. This only makes me reek of garlic. I follow the advice of my intersectional feminist Facebook group, VagChat, and douche with diluted tea tree oil, which burns like napalm. I'm halfway through drinking a bottle of apple cider vinegar. We find out that yeast likes to hide in the warm, moist folds of Aaron's foreskin. He develops a cheesy buildup and a rash of tiny abscesses on his head. Against my advice, he washes it and applies antibiotic ointment. The water feeds the fungus while the ointment suffocates and irritates the rash. We both get on a steady regimen of Monistat, him applying the soothing ointment that comes in my twenty-five-dollar kit, me penetrating myself three times a day with a plastic tube filled with chalky cream. He asks me multiple times if I'm sure it's a yeast infection. "What are you implying?" I say.

I squat in the tub to clean myself, the "whore's bath." I apply fresh Monistat cream from the shared tube in our toothbrush holder. I can tell something is wrong as soon as I leave the bathroom because Aaron doesn't immediately greet me. Usually, even if we have only been apart for a few minutes, he acknowledges me when he sees me again, like a domestic animal, but he doesn't even look at me. He's sitting on the love seat with my laptop open on the coffee table, my email up on the screen. He's naked because he wants his dick to dry out, to help the fungus die.

"I have a confession, Nina," he says. He sits forward on his elbows and turns to me. He looks somber and resolute. "When you were in the bathroom, I searched your email. It's not something I'm proud of and I'll never do it again." His voice is calm, which means he's suppressing violent urges. "Why Daniel?" he says.

"I don't know what you're talking about."

"I saw the email you wrote him." He slams my laptop closed.

"I didn't send that because I never even finished it. We literally slept, Aaron. We were sleeping in the same bed together. Asleep."

"Please don't insult me."

"It was two weeks after my abortion. I was suicidal. You were at your parents' house. I was alone. I saw Daniel at the bar. He gave me a Xanax, and I fell asleep at their apartment. Nothing happened. We didn't even touch each other."

He grips the table and pounds his head against it. I run to him and place my hand in the way.

"I was depressed, too!" he says. "Why didn't you talk to me?" His forehead is bright red, split by the vein. "I could have used someone to talk to. My mother had just had surgery."

"I did talk to you."

He pushes me out of the way and lifts a chair from the kitchen. He slams it down on the tile, and it breaks into pieces that fly around the room. "Why am I not enough?" he screams.

"You're insane."

"Punch me." He takes off his glasses and shoves his face into mine. "Punch me, I know you want to. Just do it, Nina. Just hit me. Hit me."

He points at his face.

"Fucking hit me."

"I hate you," I say.

"Hit me, then!" I back away. "Come on!" He follows me to the bathroom, and I slam the door in his face.

"It's okay, Nina! I know you want to! Just do it!"

We never fixed the door's lock; he forces it open. I push his face away and hear something crash behind him.

"You hit your partner!" he says.

I slam the door as hard as I can and scream into it, a long, open scream that swallows everything. I want our neighbors to think he's murdering me. I want the police to take him away in handcuffs. I would laugh as they were doing it.

"You're going to kill me!" I say.

He kicks through the cheap wood, and I sit with my back to it, feet wedged against the bathtub, while he kicks it again.

"Is this a yeast infection?" he says.

Bang-bang.

"Why is my dick rotting, Nina?"

Bang-bang-bang.

He throws his weight against the door and it opens each time, and I take the blows into my body, pushing harder against him. "Stop it!" I scream. I pray for a neighbor to hear me. I push harder against the bathtub with my feet. He throws himself against the door again and again. My foot slips. The edge of the wood cuts my cheek. Aaron drives the knob into my head.

twenty-one

The subject line says, *Dara sent me this.* Because of course the cells of my body vibrate at the same frequency as my mother's. The email's rambling and bleeding, almost as long as the one I sent her a few months ago. I read Dara's message at the bookstore, hunched over a Cup Noodles at the receiving-area computer. I'm wearing an eye patch, so I have to squint up close to the screen to make out the letters with my left eye only. *I don't mean to hurt you but I know I'm disappointing you,* it says. *You said I don't stick up for you or myself, but that's not true. I just struggle with you interfering in my friendships. I know you aren't the whole reason my friendship ended with Jamie (I shouldn't have said that) but I have a huge issue with you trying to control my friendship with Pam. I can't believe you think it's okay to voice your opinion to my friend about my relationship with them.*

My mother is presently traveling to her godfather's funeral. Her godfather is the only man in my mother's life who has never disappointed her, who believed her about Bruce when her parents didn't. On top of that, it's her birthday tomorrow and she hates her birthday, because although my nana planned elaborate parties for Bruce and Jude, she never celebrated her daughter. My mother is always a hosebeast around her birthday.

"Come visit us in New York," I said on our last call. "We'll celebrate here."

"I'm not going to 'visit us,'" said my mother. "I've told you, I don't know any 'us.' I know you, my daughter. I do not know Aaron because I was not given the chance to know Aaron, so I do not have a relationship with Aaron. Maybe I would visit you, but I would not be visiting Aaron."

"It seems like Dara just wants you to like her friends," I tell her now. I've gone outside to smoke and am sitting on a step by the receiving door. Across the street, in the nook of some stairs to an upscale doorknob showroom, a black kitten roots through a paper takeout bag. "People's friends are very important to them, Mom."

"Pam was competitive with me," she says. "It hurts that Dara would be friends with someone who danced with her like that in front of me."

I never know in these moments whether to validate her feelings or gently urge her in a healthier, less possessive direction. "I hear you," I say.

"How are you feeling?"

"I'm okay. I'm trying a diet I found online where I don't eat long-chain carbohydrates. It's supposed to help with my IBS."

"I remember when you stayed with me when you first got out of rehab. You had this special food that you brought with you in a lunch box. You were acting really weird about it, measuring it all out."

"That was my meal plan, Mom. They put me on a meal plan in rehab because I was bulimic."

She's forgotten that I didn't stay overnight with her. I visited her at the nudist colony for one afternoon, then left, nauseated by her polycule's family photos hanging in the hallway. I'd only come because I knew her polycule would be out of town that weekend. We sat by the pool, and I pretended not to be staring at her next-door neighbor mowing his lawn, the way his dick swung in the sun.

"Is that why you were shitting with the door open?" she says.

"Yeah, it's called accountability."

"That's exactly what I'm talking about, accountability. It hurts that Dara feels like she has to lie to me about her friendship with Pam. She went to the bathroom last night and left her phone on the nightstand. She got a text from Pam and I opened it, and they were obviously in the middle of a conversation but all their other texts had been erased."

"You snooped through her texts?"

"I didn't snoop through her texts. I read that one conversation because she left her phone out and she doesn't have a lock screen."

"That's still a violation."

"She doesn't care."

The kitten backs out of the takeout bag with a hot dog bun in its mouth. The bun is soggy with ketchup that smears all over the cat's face.

"If she doesn't care, then why would she delete all her other texts?"

"She thinks I'm going to be mad at her for hanging out with Pam."

"And you are."

"Of course I am. She lied to me."

"Honestly, Mom, I don't like you in this relationship."

"That's what Georgina and Paul say. They miss me because I have to spend all of my time with Dara. She called out of work for me the other day. *For* me. She told them I was sick. She just wanted to take me to Disney. Georgina couldn't believe it when I told her. I was standing in the open garage screaming at Dara on the phone. Just screaming my face off. I look over, and the old lady next door has stopped taking her trash out to watch me. She looked terrified." She's cackling.

"You can leave anytime," I say.

"I didn't ask you for advice."

"Okay. Why are you telling me this, then?"

"I want you to listen."

"I'm not your emotional dumpster."

"I'm sorry my problems are too much for you. You asked how I was doing and I told you honestly. I just don't need your advice."

"What's that supposed to mean?"

"It means Butters was probably someone's cat, Nina."

"What? Butters was a stray."

"Cats are very curious. Our neighbor's cat comes into our yard all the time. If I didn't know better, I might think it was a stray."

"Butters was scrawny and covered in fleas. She wanted to belong to someone."

"Did you take her to the vet?"

"Can you stop? What does this have to do with Dara?"

"You're so fucking selfish and irresponsible."

I hang up. I am giddy as I block her. "I'm never speaking to my mother again," I say cheerfully, almost proudly, to the other bookseller when I return to the registers. I send out an all-staff email telling everyone to lie to my mother if she calls the store looking for me. They already pity me. When the better Nina asked what my eye patch was for, I told her I was mugged, then pulled it down to show her the lake of blood that's filled in the western region of my eyeball, turning its whiteness red.

WE HAVE BEDBUGS. We discover them after a line of welts appears on my back, inflamed and itching, each larger than a silver dollar.

"I don't have any," says Aaron, showing me his lily-white skin, his tone suggesting that what I know in and on my very body is probably imaginary. I turn over our box spring and rip the fabric from the bottom, and live bugs come spilling out across the floor among tiny white pellets of eggs. The nearest book is William Gass's *On Being Blue*, so I grab it and start crushing them. They're clumsy, and blind, and flat, and they fall between the floorboards, into the hollows, out of my reach.

On the phone, we're told that in order to be completely certain the infestation is eradicated we will have to throw out our library. My library. I've discovered that Aaron doesn't like to read. He'll read things online, is adept at slipping into a Wikipedia hole and the deeper pages of *IndieWire*, but he hasn't read a novel since college, when he consumed all of Charles Bukowski in one semester. The only books Aaron owns are *Factotum*, *Women*, and *Love Is a Dog from Hell*, plus whatever I bring him home from the bookstore—so far a history of the Oneida sex cult and *Scar Tissue*, Anthony Kiedis's memoir. Aaron is now writing a script loosely based on Kiedis's life, blended with elements of his own. It's a period piece.

Even if I do get rid of my books, we find out, there's really no guarantee we'll be rid of the bedbugs because "they can travel through the walls from apartment to apartment," says the exterminator, now standing in our bedbug-infested studio to carry out his inspection. Our building consists of seven floors, with eight units on each floor. Some tenants have been here forty years, I tell him. "Some of them probably know they have bedbugs and don't care," he says. He explains in great detail how poison kills them by destroying the waxy coating around the bedbug, causing it to slowly desiccate and die. "We also add a gel that they walk through that shuts down certain biological functions," he says.

"Do you ever feel bad for them?" says Aaron.

"No," he says. "They outnumber us probably a million to one."

"Are you serious?" I say.

"Each female lays up to five hundred eggs. They can go for up to a year without feeding. I enjoy killing them."

"Will the pesticide hurt our plants?" says Aaron. Lately he's been pouring extra attention into the plants, overcorrecting for our last fight. He sends me updates about the plants when I'm at work, as if they're our children, as he's home all day unemployed and otherwise feels useless. In place of working regularly, even part-time, he has made of himself a housewife. The apartment is his domain, and in addition to not trusting me to cook independently, he now also doesn't trust me to water the plants appropriately. If I try to water one of them, he tells me it's the wrong day for "that guy." He's given each plant a name. My favorite is Bolígrafo, the money tree, because I named it and therefore feel some ownership over it.

THAT NIGHT, I page through every book on my bookshelves. I'm looking for any sign of activity: carcasses, pellets, brown bloodstains. I kneel on the floor while Aaron sits on the love seat above me, complaining about the hassle of having to do everything he's actively not doing. Eight bags of laundry sit in our kitchen, ready to be hauled down the street and washed then dried for an hour on high heat. He begins reading aloud about bedbugs, as if any further research is necessary after questioning the exterminator. "They mate through traumatic insemination," Aaron informs me. "The male stabs the female in the abdomen with his needle penis."

It takes me until three in the morning to put every book I own into plastic garbage bags that I double-knot at the top in an attempt to suffocate the bugs. There's nothing more I can do to sanitize the books because we don't own a microwave, but I can't let go of them, either—I've spent the year since moving into the studio building up my library after leaving most of my books on the curb in Bed-Stuy. There was no room for them at Leonard's.

I harass Aaron into helping me carry the rest of the bags down the street to the twenty-four-hour laundry. We're there until eight o'clock on the morning of the election. I stop at our local library on my way to the train and find a group of granola-eaters lined up against the outdoor wall mural depicting multicultural paper dolls connected at the hands. We greet each other over their children's strollers. The sun rises. I begrudgingly vote for Clinton.

twenty-two

We stay at Aaron's parents' house on Staten Island while an exterminator goes through our apartment and douses everything with
neurotoxins. Aaron's parents' new Maltipoo is untrained, so there
are wee-wee pads all over the floor. Everyone in the house is pretty
confident about where we each think this election is going. I suspect
Aaron's father voted for Trump, but he isn't admitting it. He would
never vote for Hillary. He keeps his eyes trained on Fox News. He's
stroking the Maltipoo and gently kissing her on the mouth over and
over. As a first-generation assimilationist with land-owning parents,
Aaron's father admires Trump's xenophobia and rabid individual-
ism. He likes to think of himself as a businessman. I watch him bliss
out as the numbers climb, as my hope sinks, then disperses entirely.
I think the new dog may be the only thing in this world that brings
Aaron's father any true happiness. He falls asleep each night holding
her beside Aaron's mother, whom he never touches in front of us. I
imagine my rage concentrating into a tight ball, becoming a cancer
growing in the center of Aaron's father's brain.

I go upstairs around midnight and stare at the ceiling with the
lights off. I feel the earth turning beneath me into a new epoch in
which perdition is actualized and the meek die under gunfire, starvation, acid rain. Aaron comes in and lies down beside me in the dark.
He can tell I'm upset, so he whispers to me as if I'm a child.

"I'm not that worried."

"Of course you're not," I say. "What do you have to worry about?"

"What do *you* have to worry about?"

"My reproductive health. My mother. Nuclear war. Our future children. Every animal species. Everyone who isn't a millionaire. Every nonwhite person I know."

"You're being dramatic," he says. "The president doesn't have that much power."

I sit up and look at him: a shart stain on the tighty-whities of humanity. Lying here in his childhood bedroom, light spilling in from the hallway, he looks like a prepubescent Boy Scout who's never controlled an erection. Aaron hated his childhood. "I was powerless," he's told me. He hated the limitations of his body and brain; hated and rejected the idea that he didn't know everything. He resented any restrictions placed on his movement or his personal achievements, others' failures to recognize and reward his genius. Aaron is ashamed that he ever was a child, derives no pleasure from remembering it. He hates asking for permission, for instance to use his father's Netflix log-in. He hates having to ask me for money. It reminds him that even in his adulthood, he is in so many ways still such a fucking child. He refers to his twenties as the "prolonged adolescence of the artist." Yet he believes that if others are struggling, it's due to their failure.

"Who did you vote for?" I say.

"I didn't vote."

"What?"

"I didn't have time."

"You had all day, Aaron. The library is down the street."

"I was waiting for the exterminator."

"He came at three o'clock. You could have gone at any time."

"What's the point?" he says. "It makes no difference. It's a rigged system. I don't even like either candidate."

"I hate you," I say, standing from the bed. I throw the lights on and begin packing my suitcase. "I truly hate you and I want a divorce."

"Can you stop saying that every time we argue? It hurts my feelings."

"Good," I say. "I'm glad you're in pain. I want you to be in pain. It amazes me that you even have feelings."

"That's not fair."

"You know what's not fair? Our country just elected someone who thinks it's okay to grab women by their genitals. Who brags about it."

"And that's my fault? You're being ridiculous. Where are you going?"

"That's none of your business anymore."

"Our house is full of bug spray."

"I don't care. I'd rather die than stay here with you."

"Will you just calm down?"

"Has that ever worked?" I say, chucking a pair of shoes at his head. He blocks them with his forearms. "In the history of humanity, has it ever worked to tell a woman to *fucking* calm down?"

I jump on the bed and start mashing the pillows into his face. He screams. I knee him in the jaw and then march across the room to pick up the shoes, throwing them as hard as I can toward my suitcase.

"You're insane," he says.

"And you're a piece of shit," I say, sticking my finger in his face. He covers himself as if I'm going to hit him. "Don't ever talk to me again, you privileged, useless prick, you're a *fucking* embarrassment."

I STAND ON the sidewalk wrapped in my jacket waiting for my Uber. It's one in the morning, and TVs flicker behind curtains down the street. The sounds of white people celebrating light up Staten Island. I am crying softly. Ten miles from here, the Fresh Kills Landfill is seeping through the ground and poisoning everything in its midst. It was once the largest landfill and the largest man-made structure. I'm half a mile from the corner where Eric Garner told Daniel Pantaleo, an officer who pledged to be faithful to him unto death, ten times that he couldn't breathe, before passing out forever. Two figures smoke on the porch across from me, watching.

Aaron comes outside. "Nina, stop yelling."

"Shut the fuck up, Aaron."

"This is what I'm talking about. Am I not allowed to have my own opinion?"

"I'm aware of your opinion and I want nothing to do with you."

"I wish we could talk about this maturely."

"Me, too. I wish you were any kind of man."

"I know what this is really about."

"Do you."

"You can't be monogamous. I was thinking about it just now, and it's just not how you're made. Your mom is a slut. Right? I think it's genetic."

"Fuck you, you're basically a virgin."

"Please stop yelling at me."

"I'm not yelling. This is how I talk because I hate you."

A white SUV rounds the corner and its lights sweep over Aaron's face, blinding him. I wave my hands. It stops beside us, and Aaron jumps in front of the door.

"Get the fuck out of my way."

"Please stop yelling. People are sleeping."

"Fuck you, Aaron, get the fuck out of my way. Get the fuck out of my way. Get the fuck out of my way. Move. Move. Move."

My Uber driver calls me from inside the car beside us. Aaron takes the phone from my hand. He holds it out of my reach.

"Fuck you, Aaron!"

The phone stops ringing. The Uber starts to pull away, and I grab Aaron's shirt and shove him onto the grass. I grab my bag and run toward the Uber and open the door, rolling inside, and lock the door behind me.

MY COWORKER IS the only person I feel certain will answer the phone. She's the only one I've told about the true origin of my bloody eyeball. I told her because I saw the way she looked at me when she had to look me in the eye. Like she already knew. The red has faded into a watery brown like the stains in my underwear at the end of my period. She holds my head as I cry. She pulls her fingers through my hair. She brings me to her bed and presses me into her chest. She tells me to let it out, and she kisses my eyelids.

"Aaron screams at me. He screams when I'm lying in bed. He breaks tables, chairs, the kitchen spoon, the lightbulbs. He broke the window with his head. He picks fights with me when I'm just looking out the window of the car, he's like, 'I'm not your chauffeur.'

"This one time, he had strep throat," I tell her. Her eyes are on me as I try to convey what happened. "We drive to the hospital. It's three in the morning and Aaron's strep throat has come on fast and is really painful. We go to Maimonides. It's closest, but the emergency room has a long wait, and it's hot and smelly, with rude nurses, and it's understaffed because it's the middle of the night."

I sob for a minute.

"We wait two hours and then we decide to go somewhere else. By now, Aaron's pain has grown unbearable—he has a low tolerance for pain—and he drives maniacally. He runs red lights and stop signs. I beg him to slow down because he's scaring me and he just ignores me.

"We get to the second hospital and he pulls into the garage, and he's ready for a fight with the attendant because he knows she's going to make him pay, and he doesn't have any money. I do, but he's refusing it on principle. He thinks because he wants to, she should let him park there. He screams at her. He throws the car into reverse and we screech backwards into the street.

"He throws the car back into drive and I scream and plead with him to stop but he won't. We get to a stop sign and I jump out and go running down the block. Aaron speeds away. I'm next to the hospital, but I don't know where to go, and it's early in the morning. I'm alone, lost, scared."

I cry.

"I wander around for a minute and I see Aaron coming down the street. He gets to within a block of me and I see that he's running, and he looks at me and screams, 'Why are you crying?' Then he runs on without me.

"I stand there crying for another few minutes, then follow him inside because I don't know what else to do. He's checked in at the nurses' window and is waiting to be triaged. He's calm and acts like nothing happened. He says, 'Hey, sweetie,' when he sees me. He asks me again why I'm crying. He's actually curious.

"I just look at him in shock. He makes such a fuss about the throat swab hurting that the doctor storms away and refuses to treat him, so I have to beg the doctor to come back.

"Three days later, after telling me that he's going to quit smoking, and knowing that I hate it when he smokes inside, and knowing how terrorized I am still from the ER trip, and using my money to buy them, Aaron smokes an American Spirit in our living room right in front of me."

SETH IS SITTING on the planter outside the bookstore the next morning. He's let his new girlfriend cut his hair and is wearing one of those bike-messenger hats that make everyone look like a penis; the effect is especially pronounced on his especially big head. "Hello, Nina," he says, and there's something self-satisfied in it, as if he's glad to see me surprised, has even been anticipating it.

"Oh, hi," I say, like I've been expecting this moment, too, refusing to give him any satisfaction. I knew all along he would come for me. I know that he came here to gloat.

"You're looking healthy," he says.

"Thank you."

"I saw Odessa the other day," he says.

"Oh, how is she?"

"She's good."

"Did you see the baby?"

"I did."

He smiles and says nothing more about this. I see in his eyes that he's smiling at the memory of the baby. I suddenly want him to touch me.

"I hear you're married now," he says.

"I am."

"Don't fuck it up."

DANIEL'S SPONSOR HAS found him in a hotel room. "There was blood everywhere," Aaron tells me on the phone. I picture him flaying his wrists or spending long hours cutting his thighs before shooting himself in the mouth. Daniel did it by drinking enough in one night to kill himself, Aaron says.

I look up how much a person would have to drink to kill himself. The way it would kill him. I'm curious to know whether there's any blood. Aaron didn't specify the source of the blood. I need to know where it came from. Maybe he bled from his stomach, but this would be internal. It's possible some came out his ass.

"HE WAS GETTING drunk every night in fancy hotel rooms, traveling up and down the East Coast like a farewell tour," Aaron says. I'm sitting beside him on our rust-colored stoop. I'm holding his hand because it seems like the right thing to do. He tells me he doesn't know exactly how Daniel died—whether it was intentional or not.

"He was hemorrhaging the ten thousand dollars he'd inherited from his parents."

"The hotel room was five hundred dollars a night," I say. "I looked it up."

"I wish I had ten thousand dollars."

"Last time I saw him, he was sleeping on the floor of someone's studio," I say.

"When was that?"

"I don't remember."

"Yes, you do."

Maybe Daniel's blood was splattered across the walls and had soaked through the light blue bedspread. Maybe there was blood everywhere because Daniel had been cutting himself while drinking himself to death. Maybe the blood had nothing to do with the moment of death. Maybe he suffered for a long time before he died.

Maybe the blood and vomit only mixed outside of Daniel's body. Maybe he died in the bathtub. Maybe the blood and vomit pooled on the tile floor of the bathroom. I feel that his energy was heavy and thick like cement. I feel it grinding like tectonic plates.

Hi, Nina . . . he'd said, in his last voicemail, from two months ago. I play it for Aaron now. *It's Daniel. And, goodness, it feels like centuries. But I said I would call, and I . . .*

. . .

*. . . I would like to speak to you for—*he chuckles—*various or unknown reasons. But if you'd like to call me back, my number is 919-559-8594, and yes, I understand that in modern times, you will probably receive that, but . . . I'd love to talk to you or Aaron soon. Um . . .*

. . .

. . . Yeah, call me back, if you'd like. Okay, bye.

"I didn't," I say.

"You weren't his friend," says Aaron.

"Yes, I was."

I let go of his hand.

"Listen, Nina," he says.

I watch a woman exit her apartment across the street. She's balancing an overfull bag of laundry on her shoulder. She wobbles down the steps, and a bottle of Free & Clear detergent tumbles out of it, followed by several intimates. The detergent tumbles into the gutter and breaks open.

Aaron looks down at my hand. He places his on top of it.

"I think people can change," he says.

Acknowledgments

Eternal thanks to Patty Cottrell, Adriann Ranta Zurhellen, Erin Wicks, Rachel Hurn, Arielle Stevenson, my parents, the team at Harper, and the Ucross Foundation, without which this book would not exist.

About the Author

SARAH GERARD is the author of the essay collection *Sunshine State*, which was long-listed for the PEN/Diamonstein-Spielvogel Award for the Art of the Essay, and the novel *Binary Star*, which was a finalist for the Los Angeles Times Art Seidenbaum Award for First Fiction. Her short stories, essays, interviews, and criticism have appeared in the *New York Times*, *T* magazine, *Granta*, *Baffler*, and *Vice*, and in the anthologies *Tampa Noir*, *We Can't Help It If We're from Florida*, and *Small Blows Against Encroaching Totalitarianism*. She lives in New York City with her true love, the writer Patty Yumi Cottrell. Find her at Sarah-Gerard.com.